Incomplete Knowledge

When Fear Meets Courage

A Murder Mystery by
Merrill J. Davies

© 2025
Published in the United States by Nurturing Faith, Macon, GA.
Nurturing Faith is a book imprint of Good Faith Media (goodfaithmedia.org).
Library of Congress Cataloging-in-Publication Data is available.

ISBN: 978-1-63528-262-7

"Fear is incomplete knowledge."
Death Comes as the End
—Agatha Christie

Chapter 1

One week before her school's summer break, Eloise Erickson awoke on Saturday to the sound of sirens on the streets of Nashville. As she became aware that she was not dreaming, she looked around her small bedroom and realized one simple fact: she was totally alone. No husband, no parents, no siblings, no children. Fear of the unknown enveloped her and became her constant companion.

After only four years of marriage, she remembered the end of it vividly. "You are not what I need at this time," Eddie had said. Later, she'd learned that he'd been seeing the beautiful blond woman for several months. In the following weeks, she relied on her mother's support.

"It's not your fault," her mother had said. "You did nothing wrong, and you'll find another partner someday." Although she wanted to believe her mother, she kept thinking that somehow she had not understood how to be a good wife to Eddie.

Flo Erickson had always been a good mother, but she was especially helpful as Eloise navigated divorce proceedings and made the decision to reclaim Erickson as her last name. "Since you have no children, you don't need to be stuck with that name for the rest of your life," she said.

Flo's red hair often reflected her strong opinions, and in those first few weeks she let her daughter know exactly how she felt about the wrong that had been done to her by her husband. "Not all men are like that," she said. "Your daddy loved both of us right up until cancer took his life."

After a few months, Flo and Eloise found an apartment closer to the school where Eloise taught, and moved in together, hoping to save a little money. She and her mother got along well and enjoyed many of the same things, like reading and going to the movies. But now she was all alone in the world.

Just as she was adjusting to Eddie's betrayal, his refusal to stay married, and their eventual divorce, the unthinkable happened. It was the summer of 2008 on a Friday, and she and her mother had planned to see a movie that night after Flo got off work. Flo was the office manager for a group of four doctors. Their offices were located on the outskirts of Nashville. She got off at 5:00 p.m. and was usually home around 6:00 p.m. It was getting close to

6:30 p.m., and she still wasn't home, so Eloise was beginning to wonder if they would be able to make it to the 7:00 p.m. movie.

When the phone rang, Eloise grabbed it quickly, expecting her mother's apology for having to work late—that happened rather often these days. Instead, a man's voice informed her that her mother had been killed in a crash when a transfer truck had crossed the median and hit her head-on. He assured her that they would be investigating the accident, etc., etc. The next few days were a blur for Eloise—so many details to handle and no help. Fear of what might happen to her reigned. A couple of her teacher friends from school were there almost every evening, and her friend Sophia, whom she'd known since high school days practically lived with her for the first few weeks. Gabriela, Sophia's mother, came almost every day, too, especially during the first week.

Since Eloise and her mother didn't have a church where she could have her mother's service, Gabriela arranged for her to have a little service in their church and Eloise had her mother's remains cremated. Everything was a blur. Eloise felt like she was just led around by Sophia's family, doing as she was told. When they had the service, however, she noticed the closeness of those in the little church and wished that she and her mother had that experience. If they had, she would not have felt so alone and been so afraid. Although a few of her teacher friends at school brought food during those first few days, her help had mostly come from Sophia's family and their friends at the little church.

The shock of her mother's death left Eloise depressed and in disbelief. Since school was just out, she had the summer to adjust, though she needed more time. Finally, Eloise, along with Sophia and Gabriela, got together one day and decided that she really needed counseling to help her through the crisis. Sophia took the lead in finding a reputable counseling service and helping Eloise with the process of making sure her insurance would pay for it. After several weeks of intense counseling, she felt as if she had awakened from a bad dream. Soon school would be starting back, and she needed to get ready for it. With the help and support of Sophia, Sophia's mother, and other friends, Eloise was able to return to school that fall and manage her duties acceptably. Now, it had been nearly two years since her mother's death, and she felt that her life was back to normal in many ways.

She kept replaying her mother's words toward the end of her junior year of high school. Several of her friends were planning to visit colleges that summer. "Do we need to visit colleges?" she'd asked her mother. "Will I even be able to go to college? Or will I just need to get a job to save money for later?"

"Oh, honey, you don't have to worry. I have money for your college. My former boss made sure of that."

"You mean one of the doctors?" she'd asked.

"No, I mean way before that—my boss in Hometown, where I worked before we moved to Nashville."

"Oh, okay," she'd said that night. She was so relieved to learn that she didn't have to worry about paying for college that she'd never asked about it again. She sailed through all four years of college classes, and hardly thought about the money, and her mother had barely mentioned the guy's name that night.

The question about her mother's former boss kept nagging at her though. Eloise sat up in her bed that morning, determined to find answers. First, she tried to remember the guy's name–Charles Wright. That was it! She was sure of it. Was he living or dead? She wasn't sure. It seemed like he might have died, but if he had, she could not remember when he died or what caused his death. She was only five when they moved to Nashville, and she vaguely remembered the conversation when her mother told her they were moving, but she could not remember what her mother said. Over the years, occasionally she would mention his name when something about her life in Hometown came up. Now, of course, her mother was gone—and with her, that information.

After having a leisurely breakfast, Eloise called Sophia. As usual, Sophia picked up on the second ring, sounding excited to talk to her friend. It was interesting to Eloise that during the last few years, their roles had completely changed from the time when they first met. At that time, they were both in ninth grade, but Eloise was in a very comfortable position, having been with the same group of students practically all her life, at least since first grade. Sophia had just moved to Nashville from the West Coast. From what Eloise understood, they had arrived in a Latino neighborhood on the West Coast after Sophia's mother escaped from her abusive husband in Mexico. Sophia was five at the time and she had two younger sisters. Since her mother worked all day cleaning houses, Sophia had to help out a lot in the evenings. For some reason, Eloise and Sophia bonded almost instantly, enjoying the same things, having similar goals (they both intended to teach school), and holding the same values. Eloise did not really see herself as helping Sophia, but one day Sophia began telling her about how she'd practiced Las Posadas in her community on the west coast when celebrating Jesus' birth. Eloise stared at her with a questioning look. Sophia said, "I know you have no idea what I'm talking about, but actually all Christians are called to the practice of hospitality, and that's what you do for me."

As time went on, the girls learned from each other, and soon Sophia was well-oriented to the strange school. The two continued to be good friends throughout high school. Once Sophia came to Eloise during tenth grade telling her that some of the girls were making fun of her accent. They had also made rude comments about her immigration from Mexico. She cried and cried, and Eloise kept inviting her over and telling her how much she enjoyed their friendship. Eloise even talked to a girl she knew in the group, telling her how much their behavior had hurt Sophia. Eventually things had gotten better for Sophia, but she told Eloise that their friendship had been key to her survival in high school. They had not seen much of one another during college since Eloise attended Belmont and Sophia went to the University of Tennessee in Knoxville.

After college, they both lived in Nashville and taught school, but they went their own ways. Eloise was teaching high school English, and Sophia was teaching first grade at one of the elementary schools. However, when Eddie left Eloise, Sophia was the first person she called besides her mother. That was the beginning of a change in the relationship between the two girls, now young adults. At that time, Eloise needed Sophia's help. For the first few months, Sophia almost lived at Eloise's place. Sophia was a soft-spoken, caring friend. She would not only listen while Eloise cried and sometimes went on and on about her situation, but she would console her, reminding her of the many times she had felt the same way when they were in high school. They would talk until late in the night, often with Sophia telling Eloise how important she had been during her early years in Nashville. Eloise was devastated, blaming herself for the failure of her marriage, and saying that she felt worthless. She was also afraid that she'd never find anyone else. Sophia mentioned that maybe Eloise would benefit by talking to a professional counselor. At first, Eloise refused, saying she'd be fine. Finally, she agreed with Sophia that counseling might help when Flo joined Sophia in encouraging her to seek out someone to talk to. Soon after, she began the counseling, Eloise realized that they were right and looked forward to her sessions with the skilled counselor.

"Hello, friend," said Sophia that Saturday morning when Eloise called. "What's the plan for this wonderful Saturday? Want to get together?"

"I need some help in sorting some things out about my past. Could you come over? Maybe we could go to lunch and then come back here, and you could help me get a plan."

"Sure, I could," said Sophia without hesitation.

By the end of the day, the two of them had agreed on a plan to dig into Flo's work in the little town called Hometown in Southeast Tennessee where Eloise had lived the first five years of her life. The first task was to write a letter to a friend with whom she had kept up with at one time but had lost contact in recent years. The girl's name was Jane, and although Eloise had written to her and had letters from her all during her youth through her high school days, they had lost contact after college. Eloise thought Jane had married, but she did not have her current last name and address. She did still have Jane's parents' address, so she decided to write her a letter there, hoping the parents were still at that address and they would send it along to her.

Before long, Eloise had written a letter to Jane, asking her what she re-membered about the time when they lived in the same town. A few days later, she received a letter back from Jane. Eloise almost didn't recognize who it was from because Jane had since married and the return address said "J. Cannon" instead of Jane Darby, the name by which Eloise knew her.

Eloise tore the letter open and read:

Dear Eloise,

Thank you so much for getting in touch! It's been a while, hasn't it? So much has happened since we last communicated. When my mother gave me your letter, I was so excited once I realized it was from you. Well, first things first. As you may noticed, I have changed my name. Victor Cannon (whom you haven't met) and I married six years ago, and we have two boys, ages four and two. We do live in Hometown, but not at my mother's address! Anyway, I'd really like to see you and renew our friendship. Any chance you'll come our way sometime soon? How long has it been since we wrote to each other? I will give you my phone number at the end of the letter, and maybe you can call me sometime. I really appreciate your letter. As you can imagine, the boys keep me busy! Do you have any children? I look forward to talking with you.

In reference to your questions about what happened to Charles, I really don't know, but I have a friend who is related in some way to his family. If I could put you in contact with her, she might be able to help you. I did hear about your mother's death, and I want you to know how sorry I am about that. Let's keep in touch!

Your long-time friend,
Jane
Phone #423-555-7777

Eloise folded the letter and put it aside. In one way, the letter made her wish she could go visit, and in another way, she felt sad that her friend seemed happily married, and had no idea that her own marriage had not lasted. However, the fact that her friend knew a relative of Charles Wright made her want to learn more. It did seem strange that Jane seemed uninformed about what happened to him, but just because the town population was under 10,000 didn't mean that any one individual would know everyone in the town. She decided that she would call Jane next week, but she wanted to talk to Sophia about it first.

As soon as she told Sophia about the letter, Eloise could tell that Sophia would help her decide how to respond.

"Why don't you bring the letter over here this afternoon, and we'll talk about it?" Sophia said. "I've got to go to the store this morning, and then Mama wants me to eat lunch with her. Can you come over about 2:00 p.m.?"

That suited Eloise fine, since she looked forward to doing nothing this morning. When she arrived at Sophia's apartment, she immediately took the letter out of her purse and showed it to Sophia. "I'm glad she included her phone number, so I can actually hear her voice and get an idea about what I should do," said Eloise. "I'm also glad she knows someone who is related to Charles Wright's family."

Sophia studied the letter, rereading it two or three times. Finally, she said, "I definitely think you should call her. Maybe you should talk to her about the possibility of going back to Hometown for a visit."

"I thought about that," said Eloise. "I just feel so uncertain about meeting her now that she's married and has two kids. It may make me feel more like a failure. She didn't mention that I had my maiden name, but I am almost sure she knew that I had married, because I think that's about the time we stopped communicating—right after I married Eddie. Then I guess she must have married Victor soon after that. It sounds like she's been really busy with her two boys."

"Tell me again just what you wanted to know about Charles Wright, and why you never knew."

"Well, I'm not really sure. I guess I initially thought I wanted to talk to him because he knew Mom. But then I got to thinking that I had been told at some point that he'd died. I don't even know if he died before we moved here. I was only five, you know."

Sophia sighed. "Maybe you and your mom moved here because he died, and she had no job after that."

"Maybe. I have just always thought that Mom knew someone here, and that friend suggested we move here. But that could have been true anyway if Mom was out of a job. On the other hand, if she knew someone here, why don't I remember meeting them? Did I ever tell you that Charles Wright paid for my college?"

"No! I had no idea. In that case, I certainly understand why you would want to find out more about him," said Sophia.

"Well, it's not like he and my mom kept in touch or anything. He apparently put money in some kind of trust or something so that Mom could just keep it for my college—and she did, of course. I didn't even know about it until the summer before my senior year in high school."

"So, do you think he left it when he died or something? That would make sense," said Sophia.

"Yes, but I have no idea how or when, or even why he gave it to her. I am pretty sure they never kept in touch after we moved away. I'm so stupid I never even questioned her about it. Now I can't."

"Wow, that's amazing!" said Sophia. "He must have thought a lot of your mother."

"I guess. She did tell me that he always said he thought I was very smart and could do anything I wanted to do. Maybe he just wanted to make sure that I had the opportunity to go to college even if my mother couldn't afford it. I don't know."

Sophia looked at Eloise. "Well, all of this seems like a good mystery to me. Personally, if it were me, I'd want to find out more about the man that did that. Whether he is dead or still living, you owe it to yourself to find out a little more about who he was and why you've never known what happened to him." She stuffed the letter back in the envelope and handed it to Eloise. "Don't lose that lady's number and keep me updated on what you decide to do."

When Eloise left that afternoon, she was convinced to at least get back in touch with Jane by giving her a call.

Chapter 2

Eloise knew that she could not make a trip to Hometown before school was out, but she also knew that making a phone call might be inconvenient during those two hectic weeks before summer break. She was nervous as she dialed Jane's number on Sunday afternoon, hoping it would not be too disruptive. Maybe Jane's little boys would be napping. The phone only rang once before Jane's voice came on the line. "Hello," she said softly. Eloise recognized the voice instantly.

"I hope I'm not interrupting anything. Oh, this is Eloise."

Jane laughed. "Oh, I'd know your voice from anywhere. Even though it's another number, I just knew it was you. For one thing, I don't know anyone else in Nashville."

"I recognized your voice immediately too," Eloise admitted. "Although I did have the advantage in that I knew I was dialing your number."

They both laughed, and Jane began her usual chatter. When she paused, Eloise interjected, "Before we go any farther, I need to tell you something. I wasn't sure when we had talked or written last. I wanted to make sure that you knew that my marriage didn't work out, and I had moved back in with Mom. You said in your letter that you knew about her death."

"Yes, I heard about your mom's death," said Jane. "But I didn't know that your marriage didn't work out. I am so sorry. The last time we touched base was right before I got married, and I called to tell you I was engaged. I guess after that I got so wrapped up in my own life that I never reached out to you. I am so sorry. Whoever he was, he's the loser in that situation is all I have to say about that."

"Thank you, Jane. You are a wonderful friend."

"I'm just sorry I have not been there for you during all the troubles you've had."

"I called because I wanted to catch up, and I also had a question or two for you. I can't wait to hear all about your boys for one thing. I also had a question about the fellow that my mom worked for when we lived there. Is he still living?"

"Oh, no, I think he died either just before or just after you moved. You know we were only about four or five when you left, so I never really knew him. Charles Wright—wasn't that his name?"

"Charles Wright, yes. Well, do you think I could learn a little more about him if I came over there and stayed a few days? You said something about knowing one of his relatives. Could you put me in touch with her?"

"Sure. Rebecca Davidson—I think she's a distant cousin of Charles. I do know that she is divorced and has a daughter. We've never even talked about Charles, and I didn't know she was his cousin for a long time. At some point, someone told me, and when I asked her, she just said that she was a 'distant cousin'. Rebecca and I got to know each other when I was pregnant with my first son, and she was a nurse who lived next door." Jane stopped. "Why don't you plan to come over here sometime this summer and I'll put you in touch. She doesn't live next door anymore, but we talk often."

Eloise hesitated a moment trying to decide what to say next. "One of the reasons I wanted to find out a little more about Charles Wright was that he paid for my college. He must have either given my mother the money to start an account for my education, or he left the money when he died or something. I was never told anything about it until I was about to start my senior year in high school. My mom didn't explain, and now all I know is that he paid for my college. Of course, I can't thank him, but if I knew a little more about him or his family, it would help."

"Of course. Well, I would love to see you, and if you want to learn more about the boys, the best way to do that is to come visit us. We're here all summer because Victor is working and we won't try to take any vacation until September. Just let me know when you can come."

"Oh, that will be wonderful," said Eloise. "I'm looking at my calendar now. How about June 10? That's on a Saturday. Why don't you check with Victor and decide whether that would work? I'd probably want to be there three or four days maybe."

"I can't wait to see you! And I'd love for the boys to get to know you while they're little. I know they'll love you."

Over the last few days of the school year, Eloise tried to focus on finishing the year out, but she often thought of her upcoming trip to Hometown, where her life had begun. She remembered very little of the place, and nothing of where she had actually lived. The town was about three hours from

Nashville, she thought, and a much smaller town, but a preschooler would not notice the size of the town.

As she entered her classroom on the last day of classes, she felt excited because there were only a few more days until her trip. Final exams were in full swing. She didn't have an exam in first period, so she settled into grading and averaging as many grades as possible. A knock on her door startled her.

"Come in," she yelled.

The door opened and Ellen, one of the senior girls, came in looking rather upset. "Can I help you?" she asked.

"I don't know. I guess not, but I just wanted to talk to you, since I don't have an exam this period," she said. She sat down at a desk in front of Eloise's desk.

"Well, your high school career is over. What now? I forgot where you're going to college," said Eloise.

"That's one thing I came to tell you. My plans have changed. I thought I was going to Maryville, but it looks like I'm staying here in Nashville and going to Belmont."

Eloise could tell there was more to the story than Ellen was telling her. She looked at the young girl for a moment, trying to decide if she should ask her to explain. "Belmont seems to be a good school, maybe even better in some ways than Maryville."

"I guess so," said Ellen. Suddenly she burst into tears. Eloise allowed her to cry until she settled a little.

"Is there something you wanted to tell me about why you made that decision?" she asked.

"Well, my mom and dad are getting a divorce. My dad says he's leaving us, and Mom needs me at home to help with my little sister. She's only eight, and my mom needs me right now."

"I know this must be a big disappointment for you at this time in your life," Eloise said. "It's always hard when a family breaks up. I know it was for me when my husband left two years ago."

"I didn't know you'd been divorced," said Ellen. "I just knew you'd be a good person to talk to about anything I needed. You know you've always been my favorite teacher."

"Thank you for saying that," said Eloise. "I'll always be there for you if you need me. I've had some bad times myself. What will you major in?"

"I was actually thinking about an English major," said Ellen. "I really like to write, and I thought I might like to teach writing—maybe in college."

"I think you could do that. And don't ever forget that you've got a good friend right here in Nashville, if you ever need a person to read over your papers and give you suggestions."

"That might be just what I need when I get into studying writing," said Ellen. "You know, when I came in here, I was so upset about having to change my plans, but now I see that it might be an advantage."

"I actually know one of the professors of creative writing at Belmont. He taught in high school for a while and eventually was hired by Belmont as an adjunct, but later he went there full time. He's an excellent writer, and I think he inspires young writers."

"I know that these next few months will be difficult for our family—all of us, and I can't leave home right now. Some of my friends are saying that I should go on to Maryville, but I just can't. My mother really needs me. She's not telling me I shouldn't go, but I could be a lot more support to her if I live at home and help out with my little sister."

"That is a very mature attitude, Ellen. I'm proud of you for seeing how you can help instead of focusing only on your own needs. It'll be hard, but it's going to be hard even if you go away," said Eloise. "Know that if you need me in any way, I'll be here for you."

Ellen began to gather her things. "I must go now. Thank you so much for listening. I feel so much better now."

Chapter 3

As she entered the little town where she would visit her long-time friend, Eloise thought there was something familiar about it although she didn't exactly remember anything about the streets, stores, or houses. Somehow, she felt as if she had come home. She stopped briefly to check the exact address for Jane and Victor Cannon. They lived at 230 Brewer Street. She also found some old mail a few months ago which indicated that their own address had been on a street which she passed by on her way to the Cannon's address. It was surreal. Had she really lived in this town on that street? She stopped briefly at a stop sign and gazed down the street. It had sidewalks. She vaguely remembered running down the street to meet Jane once, their mothers reminding them to stay on the sidewalk.

When she pulled into Jane's driveway, it was late in the day—almost dark in fact. She was a bundle of nerves. She saw two little boys playing on the porch, and two adults with them. Suddenly she realized it was Jane and a man she assumed was Jane's husband.

Turning off the ignition, Eloise got out and walked quickly toward her long-time friend. Jane did not look anything like Eloise had imagined she would. She was about a head taller than Eloise, and extremely thin. She certainly did not look like she'd been pregnant twice in the last five years. Of course, neither of them could really remember what the other looked like at five years old, but Eloise had assumed Jane had gained weight because she had two little ones. That's what had happened to most of her friends who had children. Soon they were all talking at once as Jane introduced her friend to her husband and her two boys. The boys soon went back to their play, engaging their father in their games as Jane accompanied Eloise back toward the car to retrieve her luggage. As soon as they entered the guest room and began to put Eloise's luggage away, Jane said to Eloise, "I've got to tell you something about Charles Wright. He was murdered not long before you and your mother left Hometown. Another thing—they still do not know who did it."

Eloise put her hand over her mouth and sat down on the bed in total shock. "Are you sure? Where did you learn that?"

"That's what Rebecca, the woman who is a distant cousin of Charles, told me when I called her about your upcoming visit. There's also a lot more about him that I had never heard. I just think it's awful that they never caught the killer. I hope you can dig up some things that might lead them to find the killer. I can't believe they never found who did it."

Eloise sighed. "Well, now I've already learned more than I ever thought I'd learn. Do you think I will be able to meet with this cousin of his?"

"Oh yes. She said for us to call her when you got here, and we'd work out a time for you to meet her and talk."

"That's great. I really appreciate your help on this. After Mom died, there were just so many questions about the past. I don't know why I never thought to ask them while she was with me, especially after my divorce. You know, I guess I just thought she'd always be there. And then she wasn't."

"Well, I guess that's just the way most of us would do. My mother always says that there were many things she wishes she had asked her parents about too. And I'll probably do the same. One thing I think about often since your mother died is how fortunate I am to have my mother still with me. She's so much help with the boys."

"I'm sure she is. I don't remember anything much about her except the few things you have said in your letters over the years. I believe she's a nurse?"

"Yes. She works at the hospital here, but when Ben was born, she cut back on her hours some so she could help out with him on Fridays. It helps me so much, especially since Jason came along just two years later."

Eloise looked at Jane, wondering what it must be like to have a husband, two children, and a mother to help out. "You certainly are fortunate, Jane, to have a family. I never thought much about the fact that the only family mother and I had was each other until she died. Now it's just me. I have no family. I feel like I'm way behind, too. Here you are, settled into married life, motherhood, and I'm just still like I was when I graduated from college."

"I've certainly been very fortunate. My life has moved along smoothly, marrying, beginning a family with the support of my parents. I am so impressed that you've been through so much pain and yet you seem so strong and capable. I don't know if I could have done it."

"I have had to rely on some good friends to help me, for sure. One thing I had never thought about is how much fear you have when you're all alone in the world. That's one reason I wanted to come back here and learn a little about the town and the people. I just needed to come."

Eloise and Jane talked long into the night, getting caught up on all the things they had experienced in their lives. Jane had stopped working when

Ben was born, but she planned to return at some point when the boys were older. She had worked as an ex-ray technician for a few years before the boys were born, and she intended to return to work at some time when they were in school.

As they talked that night, Eloise realized that Jane was a very traditional wife and mother, doing what she was supposed to do. In one way, Eloise envied her, but in another way, she wanted to be a little different. Maybe that kind of life was not right for her, but she didn't know what kind of life she wanted. All she knew was that she wanted to be a part of something, bigger than herself. Maybe a church, a school, a community? It scared her to be all alone in the world.

The next morning, she was awake early and excited to meet Rebecca, at 10:00 a.m. as they had agreed. She was hoping to learn more about the man who had financed her college education. She felt that learning about Charles Wright would somehow be the link to her past. Rebecca had suggested they meet at the local coffee shop, which she thought would allow them to talk without too much noise.

When Eloise arrived at the coffee shop, she saw a middle-aged lady seated by herself that she thought was probably Rebecca. The lady's hair was dark, with a few grey streaks showing through, and she was reading the newspaper. Approaching her from the side, Eloise said, "Rebecca?"

Turning around with a smile, the lady said, "Yes. You must be Eloise!"

"I am. Thank you for meeting me today."

"You're welcome. I know you think we've never met, but actually I remember you as a little blond-haired preschooler the few times I went to Charles' office in the late afternoon. Of course I would not have recognized you, as you can imagine. Would you like some coffee or a muffin?" she asked as she pointed toward her own snack.

"Well, maybe some black coffee, but nothing to eat. I'll run over here and put in my order." Eloise walked over to the counter to order, aware of Rebecca's attentive eyes to her every move.

When she returned, Rebecca said, "I understand you want to know more about Charles, and I know Jane probably told you about his horrible death. Until she told me you knew nothing about his death, I assumed that you were aware of what had happened to him. What exactly do you want to know? So much happened about that time, and you know I'm not a really close relative and had not lived here long at the time of his death. I told Jane that I'm Charles' cousin, but I'm not a close relative because there are no close relatives."

"What I want to know has nothing to do with Charles' death or even his family. I don't know if Jane told you this, but my mother was killed in a car accident about two years ago, and I realized there were some things I should have asked her about, but never did, and now I can't. When I was a junior in high school, she told me her former boss–Charles, of course–had paid for my college. I was shocked because she had not told me before, but looking back on it after her death, I wish I had asked her how that came about. At the time, I knew nothing of his death, so I wondered why he did that. Like many teenagers, however, I didn't ask her to explain. The more I thought about it after her death, the more I wanted to understand. It was such a wonderful gift to me, and I began wanting to come and thank him or his family. You see, my mother worked all the time, but she would not have been able to educate me on her own."

Rebecca smiled. "The problem is I don't know if we'll ever be able to really answer that question. Like I said, I'm not a close relative, and I've never been close to Charles. In fact, I never knew him well. I went over to his office a few times when I was visiting with a friend while in college. His insurance office was not far from her parents' home, so my friend and I stopped over there a few times for some reason. I can't even remember why. She actually knew him better than I did. I do remember you, just because you were a little preschooler playing in the floor by your mother's desk."

"Do you remember when we left? Was it before or after his death?"

"Oh, it was after. In fact, it seems that he may have left part of the agency to your mother, so she worked there until she sold her part to someone else. They actually closed the office for a short time, and I think that may have been when your mother decided to move to Nashville."

"Do you think my mother just kept the money and considered that my ticket to college, or was there something else?"

"I really don't know. I wish I could be of more help, but I guess Jane thought I knew more than I did, since I told her I was his cousin."

"Is there any other person I could talk to that might know anything more? What about your friend's parents who lived here?"

"I'm not sure. My friend's parents died a few years ago. My brother Joseph might know of someone. I'll ask him and some other people in town."

"Well, I really appreciate your help. If you learn anything, let me know and I can make another trip back sometime."

As they left the coffee shop, Rebecca assured her she would try to learn something that might be of help to her. Eloise had a funny feeling she and Rebecca were linked together in some way, like they were akin to one another. She reminded herself it may have been just a feeling, but she hoped she was right.

The next day, Eloise was on her way back to Nashville. Although school was out for the summer, she was scheduled for a workshop on Monday and Tuesday. Unlike her feelings about some of the workshops she had attended, this one sounded like it might be helpful. It was all about teaching writing, her favorite subject.

Chapter 4

Eloise couldn't help feeling a little disappointed with the trip, although she was pleased with reuniting with Jane and getting to know Rebecca. She'd hoped to learn more about Charles Wright. At least Rebecca seemed committed to trying to find out more about her distant cousin. When she called Sophia after returning from Hometown that afternoon, Eloise told her all about the visit with Jane and her meeting with Rebecca. Sophia was encouraging, telling her not to give up, that Rebecca might be able to ask around and find someone who remembered more about Charles.

Early Monday morning, Eloise left her apartment and headed out to John Overton High School where the workshop was being held. John Overton was actually closer to her apartment than the school where she taught. Fortunately, she arrived early enough to have a cup of coffee and visit with a few other teachers. It was good to meet some new people before the session began. The morning session was interesting and included several opportunities to write. Before it was over, they were all assigned to a reading group. Eloise's group included another high school English teacher and two middle school English teachers. When the session broke for lunch, she made sure she got the names of the others—Sue, the high school teacher, and Wanda and Lisa, the middle school teachers. In the afternoon, the focus was on reading some professional literature on the teaching of writing. The four teachers she had been assigned to work with were to read an article, have a brief discussion of the ideas in the article, and then choose one of them to report to the class the next day. The last session for the day involved an activity where class members drew slips of paper with a career or job printed on it, and they were then paired with someone else and asked to create a dialogue between the two persons. Eloise got the word "nurse," and her partner was a "pilot." Between the two of them they were able to come up with a dialogue that both of them thought would make sense to the other teachers. Before they left for the day, they asked Sue if she would be their spokesperson the next day and agreed to meet twenty minutes early the next morning to discuss their article.

When they met the next morning, they all agreed that the idea presented in the article was a good one, and that it could be used easily in both middle school and high school. It involved having students go outdoors together and look for an object—a rock, leaf, flower, or something and write a poem about it. All four of them liked the idea and the way the writer presented it. Sue took notes as they talked about the article and she was ready to respond during the morning session.

The afternoon session was a bit shorter and involved some writing, as well as a summary of the activities of both days. Afterward, while driving home, Eloise realized that she had not thought about her trip to Hometown or Charles Wright for two days and decided that it was a good thing. She needed a break from focusing on this. Therefore, she was a little surprised when she noted that she had a message on her home phone. It was from Rebecca.

"Eloise, I just wanted you to know that when I talked to my brother Joseph, he said he'd like to talk to you, and that he might have some information that would help you. Call me when you have time."

Eloise picked up the phone immediately and called the number back. "Hello."

"Rebecca, this is Eloise Erickson. I have been participating in a two-day writing workshop for teachers and just got home and listened to your message. I wasn't sure if your call was today or yesterday because I forgot to check my messages when I got home last night."

"I called this afternoon. I don't know whether Joseph's idea will help or not, but I thought I'd tell you. He said one of the guys he works with at the School Superintendent's office had started working at that insurance office not long before Charles was killed, and he might know something since he worked closely with Charles. Would you be interested in following up on that or not?"

"Well, it's a long shot, but yes, I'd like to know if he knew anything about it."

"Do you want me to have Joseph call you? Or would you rather come over here and just set up an appointment with the guy? How would you like to handle it?"

Eloise hesitated and then said, "Why don't you have Joseph call me first, but it sounds like it would be good to set up an appointment with the guy and talk to him myself."

"Okay. I'll give Joseph your number if that's all right with you."

"That sounds like the best way to do it. That way I can get a little more information about the guy and tell Joseph when I could come over there, and I'll just let him set up an appointment for me to talk to the guy. Do you know who he is?"

"No. Joseph just referred to him as 'this guy at work.'"

"It's no problem. I just thought you might know him. All right then, I'll wait for Joseph to call."

One week later, Eloise received a call from Joseph. When she answered, Joseph said, "My sister Rebecca gave me your number. I didn't get all the information that you were trying to find out, but I work with this guy named Spencer who used to work for Charles Wright just before he was killed. In fact, I believe he was one of the people who went over to the house and saw him lying on the floor. I thought he probably knew a lot about what was going on then. I'm sure he'd be glad to talk with you, but I'm not sure how much he knows so I can't promise anything. Would you want to talk to him?"

"Rebecca told me that you knew someone who was working for Charles Wright at the time he was killed. Do you think you could set up an appointment with him if I came over there?"

"Sure. When did you want to come?"

"Well, I was looking at the week of July 7-11. Why don't you see if that guy—Spencer—could meet me sometime that week? And Joseph, I hate to ask this, but do you think I could just come to where you all work and meet him there?"

"I think so. It's the central office for the school system, so there are a lot of offices in there, and Spencer has his own office."

"That's great. Just see when he can meet with me, and I'll be there. Let me know so I can make a plan." Eloise hung up feeling like she was making a little progress.

Two days later Joseph called to say that Spencer could meet with her on Tuesday, July 8, at 2:00 in the afternoon. Joseph laughed. "Actually, he said he could meet with you anytime that day, but we came up with the time, just to be more specific."

"What do you do at the central office?" Eloise asked the question before she could stop herself. She realized it was really none of her business, but she couldn't help but wonder.

"I'm one of the assistant superintendents. I work with the science curriculum. I taught science at the middle school here in town for a while, and then I took this job about two years ago. By the way, Rebecca never told me what you do, but I got the impression you might be in education also. Are you?"

"As a matter of fact, I am an English teacher at a high school in Nashville."

"I thought you might be a teacher, because Rebecca said something about you being off during the summer."

A sharp feeling of fear overcame Eloise, and she felt a little flushed. She wasn't sure why. "I'll look forward to seeing you on July 8th when I come to meet Spencer. Could I just come to your office first and then you introduce me to him?"

"Sure. I'd be glad to," said Joseph. "I'll see you then."

Chapter 5

After a few phone calls to both Rebecca and Jane, Eloise decided to drive over to Hometown on Sunday afternoon, spend the night, and visit with Jane and her family on Monday before her appointment with Joseph's friend. Jane didn't know Joseph, but she knew of him and had seen him a few times.

"I think he's considered a 'good catch'," she said Sunday afternoon not long after Eloise arrived. She laughed. "Of course, I'm not sure you're interested in catching someone."

"I don't know either. It made me a little nervous just to talk to him on the phone last week," Eloise said. "It's been a few years since I've even considered that sort of thing. But for some reason, he made me feel glad to talk to him and at the same time a little fearful. I guess I shouldn't have reacted like that, but I did."

"Well, he has a good reputation for being a model citizen and a kind person. I knew about him when he was teaching science at the middle school. All the kids and their parents loved him there. He was a very creative teacher, according to some of the teachers at the high school who had kids at the middle school. I think they were all sorry when he was hired at the central office."

"Do you know Joseph's friend Spencer, who worked for Charles?"

Jane hesitated for a moment. "I've heard of him, but I'm not sure I've ever met him. He taught at the high school at one time, but I'm not sure what he taught. I think he must have been in the business department. Anyway, he's probably a bit older than Joseph, and I think his goal was to get into administration all the time. I remember someone saying he wasn't too happy teaching, but he liked administrative tasks and would probably do a good job at the central office."

"I look forward to meeting both these gentlemen, and I hope Spencer might remember something that would enlighten me about why Charles Wright financed my education."

The next morning, Eloise spent the morning playing with Jane's little boys. They had so much energy and were so cute. It made her wish she could have had a happy family like Jane had. The boys called her "Weese" and kept her busy—catching balls, running through the grass, and holding their hands as they walked up and down the street near their house. Soon it was getting close to lunchtime. They planned to go to the diner close by, and Eloise excused herself to get ready, having to explain everything to Ben and Jason before going upstairs.

She was relaxed as she prepared herself both for their lunch outing and to meet Joseph and Spencer later in the afternoon. When she came down the stairs, Ben and Jason were sitting on the bottom step waiting for her. "You look pretty," said Ben, "And you smell good too!"

"Thank you," she said, laughing.

"I'm sorry," said Jane. "Boys, don't bother Eloise now. It's almost time to go get some lunch."

"It's okay," said Eloise. "I haven't had this much attention in a long time."

Jane had talked with Rebecca regarding Eloise's visit and her appointment with Spencer at the Superintendent's office. Rebecca had talked with Joseph and he had agreed to pick Eloise up at Jane's at 1:30 that Tuesday, so Eloise and Jane had decided to have lunch early enough to be back home in time for the appointment.

At the diner, Jane managed to keep the boys focused on eating their food and not making a terrible mess. Eloise and Jane chatted a bit, but they were interrupted often with questions or Jane had to help the boys with their burgers and getting ketchup on their French fries.

When lunch was over, they headed back to Jane's house, and not long afterward, Jane said, "Someone is pulling into our driveway. It must be Joseph." Eloise felt her stomach tighten. Although she appreciated Jane and Rebecca arranging for Joseph to pick her up, she also wished she were driving there alone. At least she would not have felt nervous about merely getting there.

As soon as the doorbell rang, Jane went to the door and welcomed Joseph in, beginning by saying, "I'm Jane. This is my friend Eloise. We've known each other since preschool days when she lived down the street from me. Rebecca and I thought it might be easier if you could pick her up here for her appointment with Spencer."

"Oh, I am glad to do it. In fact, Rebecca didn't actually even ask me. I just volunteered." Turning to Eloise, he said, "It's nice to meet you. After our talk on the phone, I feel like I already know you!" Joseph was about six feet tall, with jet black hair, and a winning smile. His voice was soft and kind.

He did not seem to be the kind of person who drew attention to himself, but she would soon learn that he had a lot of friends.

Eloise walked over toward Jane and Joseph. "I hope this was not too much trouble. I could have driven to your office, but I do appreciate your taking time to come over here and get me."

"Oh, it was no problem to me." Looking down at his watch, he said, "Well, I guess we'd better get going. I told Spencer we'd be there by two."

"I'll see you in a while then," Eloise said, looking at Jane.

As they drove to his office, Joseph seemed a little nervous at first, but he soon began to ask Eloise questions about her memories of her early years.

"I was shocked to learn that Charles Wright had been murdered," she said.

"Yes. I did not know him well, but according to people who knew him, he was such a nice person. Have you heard the story about how he became a part of the family?"

"No, I never heard anything about him." How he became a part of the family? What does that mean?

"He was left on a doctor's doorstep at birth. He was in a basket on the front porch. I never heard much about that, but the doctor and his wife had no children, so they raised him as their son."

"Really? Did they know who left him there?" asked Eloise.

"No, not that I know of. There were rumors according to my mother, but apparently the doctor and his wife never tried to learn who had left him, so they just treated him as their child."

"That is a fascinating story itself. And then he was murdered, and they can't find out who did that either," said Eloise. "So how are you and Rebecca related to him?"

"Well, I'm not sure that we actually are related, since he was left on their doorstep, but our mom was a cousin of the doctor's wife—at least I think that's what they said. Anyway, we never knew any of them much. Mom said that she met my dad when she was in college and they married soon after that. We lived in Ohio for a long time before moving back here. Rebecca was in college by then so the two families hardly knew one another."

"Rebecca said something about coming here when she was in college to visit a friend," said Eloise. "But she didn't say anything about your parents living here."

"She may have been out of college by the time they moved back. I think I was still in middle school. Anyway, we never knew Charles' family much. I only met him a few times. The murder was in the news. I remember that."

As they pulled into the parking lot of the Superintendent's office, Joseph said, "Well, here we are. I'll take you to Spencer's office and introduce you. Then, you can come to my office when you're finished, and I'll take you back to Jane's."

By the time she got to Spencer's office, Eloise felt as if she'd known Joseph a long time. Her anxiety had subsided, and she felt comfortable enough to meet Spencer. Spencer looked up with a welcoming smile when they came in. As soon as Joseph introduced her to him, Spencer shook her hand and welcomed her into his office. She knew she'd made the right decision to come and ask this man some questions. He motioned for her to have a seat as he began to ask her about why she wanted to talk with him. He was an older man with greying hair and a quiet voice.

"So, you worked with Charles Wright?" asked Eloise. "What was he like?"

"Charles was a fine man," said Spencer. "I was just out of college at the time and was not sure what I wanted to do. I had majored in science and education, but didn't really know if teaching was my thing. He helped me to see that I could change to something else if I didn't like it. So many people had the idea that you had to stay with something once you started it, even if it was not right for you."

"Didn't you try teaching?" Eloise asked.

"Yes, but I did not find it to be my thing, so I ended up here."

"Well, I really love teaching high school English, but I think he's right about not feeling obligated to stay in any profession if it's not right for you."

"Joseph said you wanted to talk to me because I worked for Charles Wright. Rebecca told him that I might be able to answer some of your questions."

"Yes. My mother, Flo Erickson, worked for Charles when I was little, before we moved to Nashville."

Spencer sat up. "Oh yes, I remember Flo, and I remember you now. When Joseph told me that you wanted to talk to me, I'd forgotten about you, but now I remember. She brought you to the office occasionally and let you play around there for a little while until she could leave. Charles loved seeing you and he always talked about how smart you were."

Eloise smiled. "I didn't really know he'd been killed because I was only four or five at that time. I just knew that at some point Mom said we were moving. Anyway, when I got to be a junior in high school, she told me he'd paid for my college. That was a big thing for me, and I was curious about how it happened, but I never got around to asking Mom about it. Then, about two years ago she was killed in a car accident, and I realized I would never be able to ask her about it. Would you happen to know if anything was said about that while you worked there?"

"Well, that's been a while ago, but I do remember one time he had me type up some papers on a day after you'd been there. He said something about you being able to go to college, but since you were so young, I didn't think much about it. I'll bet that was it though. He may have put some money into an investment fund or something like that. It wasn't too long before he was killed."

"Do you remember much about when he was killed? Were you and my mother working the day after he died?"

Spencer shook his head. "Oh yes. I will never forget that day. Flo and I actually went over there when he didn't show up or answer his phone. We actually saw him on the floor. It was awful."

"And they never learned who did it?" asked Eloise. "Are they still looking?"

"No. It's what they call a 'cold' case now."

"You mean they aren't even trying to find the killer or killers?" she asked.

"I'm pretty sure they aren't. They've just moved on to other things I guess."

"Did they ever get any clues as to the persons or why someone would want to kill him?"

"Not really. There were lots of rumors at the time, but when they were unable to solve it, they just seemed to lose interest in the case."

"I think that's really sad that a good man like that could be killed, and they would decide that they could not find the killer. Did they not care about him?"

"Well, at the time there was a lot of talk about it and I think they tried, but eventually they just gave up. Don't get me wrong. I think they wanted to find the killer. They brought in a number of people they thought were involved or knew something about it. There was a lot of talk at the time because Charles had taken care of his mother and dad before they died and then his aunt until she died. Then he took care of some other lady. I think she might have been a lady friend of his. During all this there was a nurse who stayed over there a long time and some people thought she might have been on drugs. Anyway, she was murdered about a year before Charles. I don't think anyone was ever convicted of killing her either. There were some who thought the two murders might have been connected in some way."

"I think it's a shame they didn't find the killers of either of them," said Eloise. "What does Joseph think about it? Does he want them to re-open the case?"

"He would like for them to find the killers even now, but I don't know that he's had any luck with getting them to do it," said Spencer.

"I had no idea about all this. I wonder what Mom thought about it? She never said a word to me about any of it. Of course, I was so young at the time. She was probably afraid to say anything. Since I've learned all this, I wonder if there is any possibility that she would have known something and would have been afraid she would have been killed too. Is that a possibility?"

"I don't think so, but you might ask Joseph what he thinks. I think that she was probably like I was at the time. We just both worked at the office during the day and didn't know much about his private life."

"Well, I appreciate your meeting with me. Are you pretty sure that Charles set up some kind of fund for my college before he got killed? You don't think it was just something that was a part of her legacy at his death?" asked Eloise.

"No, I am pretty sure I typed up something for him regarding a college fund for you before he died. I remember having to put your name on it and having to verify the spelling."

"I'm not sure why I wanted that to be true, but after my mother died and I couldn't ask her about it, for some reason I wanted to learn how it came about. Thank you for telling me what you remember." Eloise gathered her purse and notepad and told Spencer she'd better go find Joseph and get going back to Jane's.

Joseph introduced her to his boss and a couple of others before they left the building. As they were getting in his car, Joseph asked her how long she planned to be in town. "I'll probably go back to Nashville tomorrow some time," she said.

"Would you be able to have dinner with me this evening?" he asked. "I feel like we haven't had much time to visit and get to know each other."

Eloise was surprised at his invitation. "I guess I could do that if you'd like to," she said. "I just thought you'd want to be rid of me, after all the trouble I've been to you today."

"Not at all," he said, smiling. "I think I could enjoy spending more time with you."

Eloise felt the heat in her face and knew she was blushing. She also felt happier than she'd felt in a long time. "Thank you," she said. Now she felt more certain that this Charles Wright had, in fact, wanted to provide for her college education. But now there was another question in her mind. Why exactly did her mother leave Hometown? Did it have anything to do with Charles Wright's murder or did she know more about it?

When she got back to Jane's and told her that she and Joseph were going to dinner that night, Jane laughed. "I told you I thought he was a good catch."

"He does seem like a nice man," Eloise admitted. She realized that for the first time in a long time, she felt good about herself. For a long time after the divorce, she'd felt like a failure. She looked forward to getting to know Joseph better, but at the same time she feared getting involved and being let down again.

Promptly at 6:00 p.m., Joseph rang Jane's doorbell. Both boys ran to the door, and Jane, holding the boys back, let him in.

Joseph looked at Eloise. "Oh, now I know why you chose to stay with Jane. So, you could play with these fellows!"

"Of course," she said. "Wouldn't you?"

"Definitely," he admitted, giving Ben a high five and tousling Jason's hair a bit. They all laughed, and the boys held onto Jane's leg, becoming shy when the spotlight was on them.

"Okay," said Joseph. "I got reservations downtown, so I guess we'd better head out."

"Have a good dinner," said Jane.

"We will. Thanks for everything," said Eloise.

When they got in the car, they were quiet for a moment as they pulled out of the driveway, and then Joseph said, "Did Spencer know anything that was helpful to you today?"

"Yes, he did. He was very helpful."

"I hope that doesn't mean you're not coming back anymore."

"Every answer seems to raise more questions. What do you know about Charles' death? I just don't understand why the case went cold."

"I've never understood that either. You know, at the time there was no one around to push them to solve it, I guess. I was just a kid, thirteen, I think. I didn't really know Charles well, and my parents, I don't think they ever really considered him family, and all of his immediate family were gone by then. So, I guess there was no one to care enough to keep asking them if they'd made any progress on the case."

"From what Spencer said today, that was a very violent crime, so you'd think people in town would have been afraid and insisted that the case be solved for the benefit of everyone. He said Charles was shot multiple times."

"Yes. And that's not all. A lady who worked for him for years was also murdered the year before. Did Spencer tell you about that?"

"He did mention something about a nurse. What did she do? You mean she worked in his office?"

"I think she worked at his home. Helped out with his aunt and that other woman. But she was not working for him at the time of her death. That's what seems strange."

"That's weird. This is a mystery that really needs to be solved," said Eloise.

The locally-owned restaurant was located on the main street going through town, and was obviously very well-liked, judging by the crowd on a weeknight. They were lucky to get a parking spot not far from the place. As they walked up the street toward the restaurant, several young people spoke to Joseph and called him by name. Eloise was impressed by this, remembering that Eddie, her ex-husband, had never liked it when students or former students approached her when they went out in the vicinity of Hillbrook High School. One young man even said to Joseph as they walked along, "Hey, Mr. Wright! Pretty lady you got with you!" Joseph just laughed and said, "Yeah, I'm doing well tonight," and walked on.

The restaurant specialized in steaks, so both Joseph and Eloise tried one that came with a salad and a baked sweet potato. As they waited for their orders, they told each other a little about their childhood, their parents, and their schooling. The atmosphere there was quiet and peaceful, so they lingered and continued to talk a while after they finished their meal.

Finally, Eloise looked at her watch. "Oh my gosh! Do you realize we've been here two hours?" she asked.

"Well, they say time flies when you're having fun, and I certainly agree. Tell me, are you interested enough in what happened to Charles to come back and dig around a little more, or are you anxious to get out of our little town?"

"I would love to, but I'd probably have to do it before school starts this fall. I would also have to have some help with it, because I'd basically only have weekends when I'm back in school."

"I'd like to help you. Would I do?"

"Of course. I was hoping you'd help me if you have the time," said Eloise.

"Charles was a good man, and since I'm sort of related to him, I would love to find the person or persons who did that to him, even if it's a little late."

When they got back to Jane's it seemed that they both kept thinking of things they needed to say, and it was obvious to Eloise that they did not want to leave one another. The time they'd spent together made her feel like she'd known Joseph for a lifetime instead of only a couple of days. Finally, she said, "I guess I really need to go in. Jane will be mortified if she sees that we're just sitting out here in the car. She'll imagine all sorts of sordid things we're doing."

Joseph laughed, and said, "Well, now why would she think that of us?"

"You know what she told me?"

"What?" asked Joseph.

"She said you were a 'good catch'!"

"Well, what do you think? Am I?"

"Maybe," Eloise said.

They both laughed, holding hands as they walked from the car to the door. "Can I call you in a few days and see when we can have you come back here?"

"You can call me anytime you want to," she said sincerely.

Jane and Eloise talked until midnight, mostly about Joseph, but Jane also had some interesting news to share about the "mystery" Eloise had decided to delve into in the next few weeks. Jane said a friend had told her there had been some talk about a rumor that a man on the police force had been involved in Charles' death in some way. Something to dig into. When the clock struck twelve, Jane said they'd better get some sleep, since her boys would be up at dawn.

Chapter 6

As soon as Eloise arrived back home, she collapsed on her bed and fell asleep. It was early evening, and when she lay down, she had thought she'd only rest a few minutes and then fix a bite to eat. The next time she awoke it was 3:00 a.m. She got up briefly and changed into her pajamas, then crawled right back in bed and stayed there until 8:00 a.m. in the morning.

After two cups of coffee and a bowl of cereal, Eloise was ready to call Sophia and report to her all that she'd done during her three-day trip. Before she could get dressed and ready to meet Sophia, her phone rang, and she saw that it was Sophia's number. As she clicked on the phone, Eloise realized that Sophia was crying. "Sophia," she said, "what is wrong? Are you all right?"

After a few sniffs, Sophia said, "Yes, I suppose so. Why do people have to be so mean?"

"They don't have to. What happened?" Eloise could imagine her beautiful dark-haired friend sitting there with tear-stained face as she related how she'd seen a group of her Mexican friends just walking down the street and suddenly five young men had come out and taunted them, threatening to hit them with baseball bats. Fortunately, a police car drove by and the men backed off and the girls got away.

Why are some people so mean? Eloise asked herself the same question often, and always she said the same thing: they don't have to be that way. There is a better way.

The two girls talked for a long time, as Eloise tried to reassure Sophia that things would be all right and told her how much their friendship meant to her. Finally, they decided to meet for lunch and spend some time together to catch up on all that had gone on while they had been apart. After lunch, Eloise finally got around to telling Sophia about meeting Joseph, talking to Spencer, and playing with Jane's little boys.

"So, it sounds like you and Joseph really got along well. Do you think you'll get together again soon?

"I'd say there's a good possibility of it," said Eloise. "He seemed to want me to come back, and he agreed to help me dig into who killed Charles Wright."

"What about the college funding? Did you learn anything about that?"

"Actually, I did. Spencer, Joseph's friend, said he was pretty sure that was set up before the murder, and he thinks he remembers typing up the papers for it. He couldn't remember anything specific, but he remembers having to get the correct spelling of my name to put on the papers."

"Well, that's progress anyway, don't you think?"

"Yes, but they never found out who killed Charles Wright, and it sounds like there was just not enough interest in the case, because he had no relatives to push it. Isn't that sad? Joseph is some sort of distant cousin, and he was excited about helping me try to get the case reopened."

"So, it sounds like this Joseph is interested in more than the murder case, huh?"

Eloise blushed. "Maybe. Listen, Joseph is a real nice guy. He's the brother of Rebecca. Remember, I told you that he was the one Rebecca told me about who had a friend at his work who had worked for Charles Wright at the time my Mom had worked there. He actually took me to the office to meet with this other guy, and then took me back to Jane's." Eloise stopped talking for a moment. "And he took me to dinner that night."

Sophia laughed. "So, he IS interested in more than solving the murder."

"Well, yeah, I guess. Like I said, he's a really nice guy, and we spent a lot of time talking and getting to know each other."

"What does he do? Is he an educator too?"

"Sort of. He doesn't teach but he works in the superintendent's office in curriculum development."

"Did you tell him you'd been married and divorced?" Eloise had told Sophia that telling a prospective "date" that she'd been married before would be the hardest thing for her to do if she had a chance to become involved again.

"Yes. That was one of the first things I told him when we started talking— thought I'd just get it out of the way."

"How did he react?"

"Oh, he just said something like 'that must've been a difficult time for you.' At the time, I had not got to know him as well as I did before I left, so I guess it was a good thing I told him early on and not at the end."

"Do you plan to go back soon?"

"I'm going back in two weeks if all goes as planned," Eloise told her. "I've got to work out where I'll stay this time. I hate to keep imposing on Jane and her family, although she'd probably let me stay. Joseph said I could probably stay with Rebecca, so I might do that."

"This is so exciting," said Sophia. "I just know you two will be right for each other. By the way, is he about your age, or how old is he?"

Eloise hesitated. "Let me see. He's a little older. I think he said he was in middle school when we left, and I was five so that would mean he's probably about nine or ten years older than I am."

"Well, that's not a bad age difference. You two could make that work," said Sophia.

Eloise looked at Sophia. "I don't know what will come of it, but I am interested in finding out who did this to Charles Wright, and Joseph is interested in that too, so I thought I may as well let him help me. We'll see what develops about our relationship, but at least I'm willing to spend some more time with him."

"I think that's wonderful," Sophia said.

"What about you, Sophia? Have you met anyone that is a possibility?" Eloise asked her.

"Not really. There's this one guy I met who lives in my apartment building, but I think he is hesitant to get involved with me, because I, you know, am from another country." Her eyes became tearful as she went on. "I always thought that if I was here all through high school, I'd be accepted. And then I thought if I was here through college, it would surely be enough. When will I be…enough?"

"The right person will come along. I'm sure of it. I think when someone gets to know you, they'll realize that you're not any different just because you were born in a different country."

"We'll see. I feel like so many people hold that against me. They think that I'm different somehow."

"Well, you and I didn't take long to become friends, did we? We always had a lot in common. It had nothing to do with where you were born or the fact you'd moved here from California. All that just added to my fascination with my new friend who understood me better than anyone else." While Eloise was talking, Sophia was looking intently at her face. When she stopped talking, Sophia had a big smile on her face.

"You're right," she said. "I felt the same way. Before I moved here, I lived in a Latino neighborhood, so I knew a lot of the kids there, and I was scared when I came here, but after I met you and we became friends, I often thought about how comfortable you made me feel. I couldn't think of a single friend back on the West Coast that understood me like you did. So maybe I will eventually meet someone, a man, that will accept me just as you did, not for where I came from, but for who I am."

"Of course you will," said Eloise. "I'm convinced of it. I went through a period when I felt like I wouldn't meet anyone after my divorce. And it may take a while, but meeting and talking with Joseph this week made me realize that maybe the failure of my marriage might not have been all my fault, and maybe I could be happy with someone and make him happy too. That's the reason I want to give our relationship a chance, even if it doesn't work out."

Eloise went back to her apartment that day feeling that she had a true friend in Sophia, and she was glad that she had been able to reciprocate for some of the help she had received from Sophia over the last two years since her mother had been gone. Sophia had been supportive in so many ways, both emotionally and in physical ways too. When Eloise moved to the new apartment, Sophia had helped her pack up to move as well as helped her get everything arranged when she moved in. Her cheerfulness had been so helpful. They had laughed as they worked, and they were often dead tired at the end of the day, but to have a friend to help was the most important part, since for a long time Eloise's mother had fulfilled that role in her life.

Chapter 7

Joseph called Eloise the week after her visit to arrange for her next visit. He told her that Rebecca would love to have her stay at their house the next time she came, and they agreed upon a date for her trip there. He told her that he would have something lined up for them to "investigate" while she was in town. She also talked to both Rebecca and Jane about her visit. Jane told her that she was happy for her to stay with them anytime she needed to, but she understood her need to stay at Rebecca's part of the time.

Eloise drove toward Hometown on a Thursday since Joseph wanted her to stay over the weekend so she could meet some of his friends who were off work during that time. He would also have more time to spend with her on Saturday and Sunday. She looked forward to getting to know him better.

As soon as she arrived, she saw Rebecca coming out to greet her. "I thought you'd never get here," she said. "I'm SO glad Joseph is involved in looking into Charles' murder. I've always thought it was not right that they never found his killer. Of course, I'm sure it'll be hard to find him now," she said as she ushered Eloise onto the porch.

"That's true, but like you, I find it difficult to accept the fact that they never found his killer," said Eloise.

"I'm really glad that Joseph finally found someone he likes to be with. I had decided he might just remain an old bachelor all his life. Isn't he a nice guy though?" Rebecca said, grinning from ear to ear, as they entered her living room.

Eloise was starting to get a little embarrassed and began wondering if this was such a good idea to be staying with Rebecca. Soon the conversation moved to other topics though, and she was feeling better. Maybe Rebecca had sensed that she'd said a little too much and chose to ease the tension she had caused. They both naturally sat down, Eloise on a chair and Rebecca on the couch. Just as Eloise started to say something, a young girl, probably in her early teens came into the living room. "Oh," said Rebecca, "this is my daughter Abby. And Abby, I guess you've already figured out that this is Eloise. Would you help her get the luggage out of the car and show her where to put it?" Looking at Eloise, she said, "Joseph said for me to call him when you got here."

"Sure," said Abby, moving toward the door as Eloise arose and followed her.

Eloise opened her trunk and handed Abby her suitcase as she simultaneously grabbed her carry-on luggage and closed the trunk. "Thank you so much for helping me," she said to Abby. The girl was obviously comfortable with adults and started asking Eloise how her trip was from Nashville. By the time they got upstairs, she had learned that Eloise was an English teacher and had told her English was her favorite subject. "What grade are you in?" asked Eloise.

"I've just finished eighth grade," said Abby. "I'll be in high school this fall—I can't wait."

"I'll bet you're a good student too," said Eloise.

"I think I'm a pretty good student," she said as Rebecca entered the room.

"Oh yes, she's a good student, Eloise, especially in the field of English and writing. She loves to read. She's never had a problem with all that."

"Well, then, you and I should get along great," Eloise said.

"Oh, Joseph is coming over. I told him the two of you are welcome to eat with us. I'm just making soup and salad, but we'd be glad to have you. Joseph said he'd just let you decide. He said to tell you he'd take you out to eat if you'd rather do that."

"Oh, soup and salad will be fine with me, if it's no trouble to you."

"Well, then it's settled," said Rebecca. "You take some time to relax a little, and Abby and I will get out of your way and start to finish up our dinner."

The guest room was simple, but nice and relaxing. Eloise put her things up and then sat down for a few minutes. Before heading downstairs, she changed into the outfit she'd brought for tonight—nothing fancy, just fresh and clean.

When she went downstairs, Abby was just finishing setting the table. They had already chopped up vegetables for the salad, and she could smell the delicious soup cooking on the stove. It had been a while since Eloise had felt the comfort of home like she did as she entered the kitchen. It reminded her of her mother's kitchen.

About fifteen minutes later, the doorbell rang, and Abby said, "It's Uncle Joseph! I'll let him in."

It was obvious that Joseph and Abby had a good relationship, comfortable and loving. It felt good to hear them teasing and talking about things they had in common, family "stuff."

The dinner was delicious. When they finished, Rebecca said, "I don't really have a dessert planned. Joseph, I thought you and Eloise might want to go down to the ice cream shop. Abby and I have been forgoing dessert this month, as we tend to have too many sweets during the week.

"That sounds like a good idea. Eloise, would that be okay with you?"

"Sure. Whatever suits you."

As they were on the way to the ice cream shop, Joseph said, "I've got an idea. Why don't we go to the newspaper office in the morning and see what they have in the way of articles in their files printed right after Charles was murdered. That way we might get some ideas about where to go from there. How does that sound?"

"I think that's a brilliant idea!" she said.

Later, as they were finishing their ice cream, Joseph asked her if she thought they should look for anything specific when they were reading the articles in the newspaper office.

"Not exactly, but we might write down the names of any persons mentioned that might lead to additional information—like the person or persons who found him, worked with him--things like that."

As they continued to talk about the articles they might find, Joseph asked, "What about any mention of anyone with whom he'd disagreed or had problems with? I've never heard of anyone who had a conflict with Charles, so it's hard to imagine that he had enemies, but I guess you never know."

"Yeah, but according to what I've heard, that's not likely to be there. Just use your own judgment, but if you see something that we might need to follow up on, make a note and then we can decide later."

By the time they left the ice cream shop, they had several ideas. Basically, they decided to read the articles and see what they could come up with. It might be that they would only see something they'd want to ask the police about when they went there.

When they got back to Rebecca's house, Joseph said he'd better go on home and not go inside. "I want you to know how much I appreciate your wanting to do this. I know I should have done it a long time ago, but for some reason I never got around to it."

"Well, when I first came, it was mostly to learn about why this person would have paid for my college, but when I learned a little more about him, it just seemed unfair not to find the truth about what happened to him,"

Eloise said. "By the way, I'm really enjoying getting to know Rebecca and Abby. Does Rebecca have a husband?"

"No. Not since Abby was two. He just wasn't a 'fatherly' type of man, I guess. Anyway, he and Rebecca started having problems right after Abby was born. He could never put anyone's needs before his own, and Rebecca was always sort of in the middle. He would want them to go somewhere for the weekend or something and Rebecca was not willing to leave Abby for very long. I don't know what all led to their eventual break-up, but by the time Abby was two they had split up. He's never paid much attention to her over the last few years."

"Does he pay Rebecca any alimony or child support?"

"No. I think Rebecca decided she'd rather take care of herself and Abby than to have to communicate with him. At first, he said he'd pay child support, but after several times not getting it, she just quit asking about it, I guess. He's moved away, and he seldom has any communication with them."

"Rebecca and I have a lot in common. I can tell that already. And she has obviously done a fantastic job raising Abby. I love her. She's an ideal kid," said Eloise. "I felt so much like I was with family tonight."

"Well, you might eventually be," said Joseph, with a grin on his face. Eloise was glad it was getting dark as they walked up to the door. "What if I pick you up around 9:30 in the morning to go to the newspaper offices? Is that okay, or would you rather I come later?"

"9:30 a.m. is fine," she said. "I'll be ready."

Friday morning, Rebecca and Eloise had a quiet breakfast on the little screened-in porch just off the kitchen while Abby slept in late. "Abby is a sweet girl," said Eloise. "I've fallen in love with her in the short time I've been here."

"She is my love," said Rebecca. "Has anyone told you that her daddy left us when she was two?"

"Joseph told me a little about it last night. You seem to have done so well with all that, but it must have been difficult."

"Yes. There were times when I didn't think I could do it. At some point though, when Abby was about four, I decided everything was going to be okay. From then on, I've managed pretty well."

"You certainly have, and to think, you have raised a wonderful young lady in the meantime," said Eloise. "I guess I'd better get upstairs and finish getting ready. Joseph said he'd come to get me around 9:30 a.m., and we're going to the newspaper to see what we can find that was written about Charles' murder."

"I can tell that Joseph likes you a lot," said Rebecca. "He hasn't shown this much interest in a lady in a long time. I know that you asked him to help you dig into Charles' murder, but I think there's more to it than that."

"Well, we'll see," said Eloise. "I've not been very interested in anyone since Eddie and I divorced either, but I do feel very comfortable around Joseph. And it doesn't hurt that I also like being around you and Abby."

"We like having you around, too." Rebecca smiled. "Joseph was hurt pretty badly a few years ago when a woman he'd been dating for some time suddenly dropped him for a guy who had a lot more money. We were all expecting that they would marry, so it hurt us all to some extent."

When Joseph picked Eloise up and they headed for the newspaper offices, she was excited to think they might learn some interesting facts about the murder.

The person who greeted them at the newspaper that morning was a young man who looked to be in his late twenties or early thirties. At first, he seemed uncertain about where they needed to look for something that happened that far back, but after consulting with someone on the phone, he quickly referred them back to the archives and told them which section to look in. He wasn't sure of the exact dates, but he knew which month to start with and assured them that there were several articles within one or two weeks.

They soon found the first article, and it was easy to find the others. The guy had told them they could pull the paper out and read any articles they needed, and that he would be glad to copy any articles or parts of articles they needed for them. Soon they both were reading and making notes from the articles.

"This article says he was shot five times in the back of his head," Joseph said. "And it also gives the names of the two people who saw him lying on the floor. It says that at first they thought he might have had a heart attack because he had some sort of heart condition."

After a few minutes, Eloise said, "Here is another article that talks about his heart condition, and it says that he had told a friend that he was planning to go to a basketball game that night, but never showed up. It doesn't give the name of the friend though. Maybe the police would know who that was. He might have more information if we could locate him. It also talks about

Charles being very devoted to taking care of a woman friend for many years who lived in another town as well as taking care of his aunt who lived here."

"Yeah, I've heard about the aunt he took care of. I think she was my dad's cousin or maybe my mother's. I forget how she was connected, but I can find out. Oh, here's an article that talks about a pastor in a church close by Charles' home that heard something he thought was firecrackers...or gun shots...on the night of the killing. I'd like to talk to him and see what he remembers."

"This article is all about leads in the case," said Eloise. "It says that the Sergeant says they've made progress in the case. It also said that they have 'numerous leads.' It goes on to say that they think it was someone who was 'very skilled' in how they went about killing him—firing into a pillow that was placed over his head. Here's something else–they think his death might be in some way connected to another killing that happened less than a year before. It has the name of that person. She worked for Charles, helping him care for that aunt."

Joseph said, "This article says that Charles had been receiving harassing phone calls. They didn't say what they were about though. They did say that one of his telephones was missing, along with his keys. I wonder why they would have taken a telephone."

"Maybe it had a message from one of those harassing calls," said Eloise.

"Interesting," said Joseph. "We might want to follow up on that."

"Now this is rather interesting," said Eloise. "It says that the autopsy found five bullet wounds in Charles' head according to the preliminary state medical examiner's office, but there were no bullet marks found in the house, though they found 11 hulls. So where did the other six bullets from the .22 calibre pistol go? They do say that they had not received the final report yet."

The other articles they looked at were editorial type pieces, showing how well Charles had been loved in the community and expressing shock that such a horrible crime had been committed in this small town. Neither Joseph nor Eloise found any reason to copy any of the articles at that time, so they left and headed down to a little diner for lunch.

"Where do we go from here?" asked Eloise when they were getting finished with lunch.

"I had hoped we might stop by the police station and ask some questions. I wonder if they have any records we could peruse, or whether they would let us dig around a bit in some of the things they'd learned. I really don't know, but I'd like to talk to them before we go any further. What do you think?"

"That's a good idea," said Eloise. "I don't want to do anything inappropriate or illegal."

"Me either. And I don't want to get you into something you'd rather not get into."

"It's actually kind of exciting, what we're doing, but I don't know what we are allowed to do. The idea that he was getting harassing phone calls in interesting. Do you know anything about why he would have been getting calls like that? Have you heard any rumors?"

"No. But it wouldn't hurt to see if the police ever learned anything about that aspect," said Joseph.

"Do you think any of the policemen that are here now would have been here back then?"

"I doubt it, but I don't know. I would think they would be retired by now."

"Why don't we make a list of a few things we'd like to ask about, mainly what we can do legally, and then go over there and talk to them a bit to see if they would have any objection," said Eloise.

"That sounds like a great idea," said Joseph. "That way, if we don't get to talk to whoever knows what we can do, at least we can find out when we might be able to talk to someone about it."

They spent about twenty minutes compiling a list of a few questions, frequently marking out some and adding others, trying to decide on a few that they felt like needed to be addressed first. Finally, they were ready to go to the local police department, both of them feeling a little uncomfortable about doing so.

The little diner where they had eaten lunch was located in the middle of town and the police department was out of town a bit, so it took them about fifteen minutes to get there. It was a new building and looked very intimidating to Eloise. "Are you sure you want to do this?" said Joseph. "We don't have to, you know."

"No, I'm all in," she said, smiling at him. "It'll impress all my teacher friends when I go back to school this fall. Even some of my students might be impressed."

Joseph laughed. "Well, I'll try not to get you arrested, so you *can*, in fact, go back to school."

"I'll try my best to avoid that. If they say it's against the law, then I won't do it. I'll operate by the book." As they walked up the steps to the front of the building, Eloise said, "By the way, just so you know, I plan to let you do the talking in here. We've talked about what we want to ask, but I want you to be the main spokesperson. Is that okay with you?"

"Of course, but don't hesitate to jump in if you think of something I'm overlooking."

"Okay. Will do. You may actually know some of the folks that work here. I'm sure I won't though."

The lady at the desk asked if she could help them, and Joseph told her that they wanted some information about a case that had gone cold several years ago. "Do you think we could talk to someone about whether there would be any evidence or something that we could look at to get a better picture of what happened?"

"I guess so. How far back does the case go?" asked the lady.

"It was a murder that happened to a relative of mine back in the eighties. I think it was 1984."

"Oh, that is way back there. Yes, they have an archive room, but I don't think I'm allowed to let anyone back there without someone with them. If you can wait a few minutes, my supervisor will be back up here, and he'll know what the rules are. Feel free to have a seat right over there if you'd like." She pointed toward a little seating area across from her desk. "He should be back in about ten or fifteen minutes. I'm sorry, but as you can imagine, I don't get that particular question very often."

"I'm sure you don't," said Joseph. "It's no problem. We'll just sit over here and relax a bit."

The sitting area was a good way over there and when they sat down, Joseph said, "Is this okay with you? I mean, you're not in a hurry, are you?"

"Oh no, I'm fine. You know the main reason I came here was to get started with this project, so I'll do whatever it takes."

"Tell me a little about why your mother worked here when you were little. Do you remember anything about being here?"

"No, I really don't remember anything at all. In fact, that's why I had so many questions about Charles Wright after my mother died. Did I tell you that he paid for my college?"

"Yes, and you said Spencer thought he remembered drawing up the papers, but did he have any idea why Charles would have done that?"

"Not really," Eloise said, "but to me it just meant that he must have been a person who cared about me and wanted me to have what I needed. After my mother died, I felt so alone. I guess that was why I had so many questions about him."

"Well, maybe he just thought it'd be a shame for a smart little girl not to have the opportunity to go to college, so he made sure you had the resources to do it," said Joseph, giving her a big grin.

Soon a middle-aged man came out from the back and said something to the lady who had talked to them earlier. They assumed she explained what they had wanted, because he then came over and introduced himself. "I'm Sergeant Jackson. I came here from Georgia two years ago. So, you're interested in the Charles Wright case. Ms. Nelson said you were a relative of his?"

"Well, a distant relative. I was a kid when this happened, and I don't really know too much about it, but I think it's a shame someone or some people got away with a horrible murder," said Joseph.

"My sentiments exactly. I've asked around here a little about why that case went cold so quickly. So far, I haven't learned much though. For one thing, no one seems to work here now who was working here back in the eighties. Of course, I'm sure there are a number of people who were living here at the time, but they didn't necessarily work here. I did learn of one man who was working here at the time who is retired now but still lives in town. I haven't met him though."

"We looked at several news articles about the murder earlier today, and got a little information," said Joseph. "Would it be possible for us to see some of the evidence and internal memos or whatever your station found at the time?"

"Sure, I can take you back to our archives, and show you some of the things I've looked at recently, and we can go from there," said Jackson.

"Oh, by the way, this is Eloise, a friend of mine from Nashville. At the time of the murder, her mother was working for Charles, but Eloise was only about five years old, so she wasn't told anything about it. She wants us to look into it."

"Well, like I said earlier, I also think it's a shame the case was never prosecuted. Of course, it's hard for me to work on it now, but if you two want to look into it, I'll be glad to help in any way I can. I also have a detective that I think might be interested from what he's said."

As they entered the archives, a chill went over Eloise. It was rather dark and a little too cool for her. When Sergeant Jackson turned on the lights, they were located along the sides of the room, which made the room continue to look a little dark. He pulled out a couple of folders filled with musty papers and then a box that held some items that Eloise couldn't identify from where she stood. "I guess the best thing for you to do initially is look through what's in these folders. "I'm glad you saw the articles from the newspaper. You may not learn too much from these, but they may help you understand what the articles said."

Jackson then said, "I've got to leave you here for a bit to make a phone call, but I clipped some of this stuff together with a note on the top to help me remember what was in it. You can see what my assessment has been in them. Also, I have put a few questions on some of the papers, and a few names that I think we should contact. I think I put a sticky note on one stack with the name and address of that guy who was working here at the time. Feel free to copy his name and address if you want to follow up on it. Now, I'll leave you to peruse all this, but I'll be back in a bit to see if you have any questions I can answer."

"This is exciting," said Eloise when he left. "And we're lucky that there is someone new here who wants to know about it too. "What do you think?"

"I feel the same way." Joseph was flipping through the notes and reports in the folder he had in front of him.

When he returned, the Sergeant had a young man with him who looked about the same age as Joseph. He introduced the young man as Detective Barrett. "This is the detective that I told you about who was also interested in this case," he said.

The young man reached out to shake their hands. "I'm Don Barrett," he said, seeming uncomfortable with being identified by his title.

"Have either of you come up with any theories of what might have been a motive for a murder like this?" asked Joseph.

"Not really, but I'm thinking it must have been a bit complicated," said Jackson. "I'm sure you read the article where they talked about the murder being committed by someone who knew what they were doing. That interested me. If that is true, then it had to have been planned in advance. It wasn't just a job that was done in a moment of anger."

By the time they left the police station that afternoon, Eloise was exhausted, and she sensed that Joseph was too.

As they pulled out of the parking lot, Joseph let out a long sigh. "Wow, that was intense, wasn't it? I think I've worn you out today."

"Well, yes, I'm exhausted, but given the fact that I can't be here all the time, I'm glad we got to do a lot today," said Eloise. "Maybe we can meet for a while before I leave tomorrow and get a plan for some things you could investigate on your own in the coming days, and then I could plan another trip over here in a few weeks before school starts. After I get back in school, the best I'll be able to do is come over on some weekends."

"I wish you could be here some during the week too. You think of things I would never think about—and I like working with you."

"I'll have a few days off for fall break sometime—probably October—so maybe that will help."

"Oh, yes, that will be great. Also, could I come visit you one weekend after school starts?" Joseph asked.

"Sure. I'd like that. I'd like you to meet my friend Sophia, too. She's been very supportive to me since my mother died. I don't know what I would have done without her, especially when I moved out of the apartment where my mom and I lived for a while."

"Sophia? Is she wise?" asked Joseph. "Her name suggests she is."

"I think she is. She and I have been friends since ninth grade when she moved to Nashville from the west coast. She's from Mexico. She and her mother and sisters escaped from an abusive father, and they had been in a Latino neighborhood since Sophia was about five. Moving to Nashville was a big step for her family, but she's done really well. She always made good grades."

"That shows that Sophia is an appropriate name for your friend," said Joseph.

"Yes, but sometimes people are unkind to her just because she is from Mexico. People can be so mean to people because they are different in some way. I wish they wouldn't do that."

Joseph put his hand on her shoulder. "But Sophia was lucky to have a friend like you. I know that. I bet you've helped her a lot."

"I hope so, but then again, she's often been a help to me too. When Eddie left me and we divorced, Sophia was there for me a lot, and then when my mom died, she was there too. It kind of seems that we've changed roles in a lot of ways. During high school, I felt like I was the helper to her, but when I started having problems, she was right there comforting me too. Her mother and sisters were too. It was like I had a real family during that time."

"That's what friends are for. It doesn't matter where you're from, or what you look like. The important thing is that you care for one another, and you're able to communicate," said Joseph.

Joseph dropped Eloise off at Rebecca's, and they agreed to meet the next morning before she left to go back to Nashville. That evening she enjoyed visiting with Rebecca and Abby and helping them clean up after dinner.

"What did you learn today?" asked Rebecca as soon as Eloise came in the door.

"Oh, lots of things. But the most interesting thing to me was that the sergeant in charge, or at least he seemed to be in charge, has actually been digging into Charles' murder case himself, and he seemed to want us to see if we could learn more about it. He said he didn't understand why it was never solved. He showed us a bunch of stuff he'd learned. It made me feel like they'd welcome our 'investigation' of the case."

"Wow! That's exciting," said Rebecca.

"Yes, it definitely is. I guess I was expecting the people at the police station to be reluctant to let us look at anything, so I was surprised that he took us down to the archives and let us spend a good bit of time looking at what he'd found and his notes about it. He actually left us to peruse all his findings for a while, and then he came back and talked to us before we left."

"Well, that's encouraging."

"I think when Joseph told him that he was related to Charles, it made him hopeful that things could be done. We also learned the name of a retired policeman who still lives here who might know more."

"All this sounds great. Will you be coming back soon to continue your investigation?" asked Rebecca.

"Joseph and I are going to meet in the morning and talk about where to go from here. I'll be leaving after we meet. I might be able to come back one more time before school starts. Then it'll be a little harder for me to get away, but we'll see."

"And what about you and Joseph? How's that going?"

"Well, I guess we'll wait and see about that too. He did ask me if he could come visit me in Nashville one weekend after school starts," Eloise said with a mischievous smile.

"And what did you say?" Rebecca asked.

"Oh, I said I would love to have him come visit and meet my friends. I told him about my friend Sophia, that I've known since ninth grade in high school. Have I told you about her?'"

"I don't think so."

"Well, Sophia is my best friend. She's from Mexico, and I know that some people are unwilling to accept people who are different, so I just wanted to make sure Joseph wasn't one of those people."

"Well, did he pass the test?"

"Oh yes, with flying colors."

"I thought he probably did. Joseph has always been one of those people who loved all people no matter where they're from. He used to quote Jesus about loving the Lord with all your heart and your neighbor as yourself. And then he'd say 'and he didn't say if they spoke your language or if they looked like you, or anything like that. He just said to love our neighbors as ourselves.' He'd get all riled up when his friends started excluding people that were different, especially if they went to church with him."

"I've always believed the same thing, so we agree on that," Eloise said.

Rebecca didn't ask any more about their relationship, and Eloise was glad because she felt it wouldn't be fair to Joseph for her to go into any depth about her feelings for him or to tell Rebecca any more about what they'd said. She realized, though, that her feelings were definitely more positive than they had been before she'd had this visit.

Chapter 8

When Eloise met Joseph for a short breakfast the next morning, they both decided that the next logical step might be for Joseph to contact Detective Barrett and see if they could both have a meeting with Philip Dubois, the guy that was working at the police station when Charles Wright was killed. From him they should be able to learn if any others who were there were still around, and he might remember some things that had happened during that time that others had forgotten. They also decided that she would come back the week before her school started back for the fall.

"I guess I'd better get on the road," said Eloise after they finished eating and had decided on these two things. "Is there anything else we needed to talk about?"

Joseph began, "Uh, well, yes there is something, but it doesn't have to do with what we've been talking about exactly," he stammered. It was unlike him to have problems saying what he wanted to, but he seemed almost embarrassed.

"Well, what is it?" she asked.

"I…I don't know how to say this, but I really like having you here, and I just wanted to know if you're seeing anyone in Nashville, because if you are, then maybe I should back off a little."

"The truth is, I'm not seeing anyone. I haven't been involved with anyone since my husband left me a few years ago—until I met you, that is," said Eloise. "I have been afraid to get involved because I've not been able to trust anyone. That may seem difficult for you to believe, but it left me feeling very vulnerable. Since I met you, however, I've realized that just because Eddie chose not to stay with me doesn't necessarily mean I'm not worthy."

"Oh, I do understand what you're saying. I had a similar experience several years ago, although it didn't get to a marriage contract. But it's the reason I'm still single. Not only did I begin to doubt my own self-worth, I also believed that I'd never be able to trust a woman again, but you're so different. Do you think we can trust each other?"

"Yes, I do," Eloise said. "What about you? Do you believe me when I tell you that I am not seeing anyone?"

"I'm beginning to trust you more all the time," he said. "You're the first person I've really enjoyed being with in a long time."

"You can contact me any time, and be sure that I'm not seeing anyone else," Eloise said.

Joseph gave her a hug before she left and told her to be safe on her way back to Nashville. She thought about their conversation as she drove back, becoming more convinced with every mile that she had found someone she could trust.

When she got back to her apartment, she called Joseph to tell him that she'd made it safely and they talked briefly about her next visit. Afterward, she called Sophia to tell her all about her trip, especially about the development between her and Joseph. When she checked her messages, she found one from her principal. He said he needed her to call him because he was trying to work out the fall schedule. Since he called her that morning and this was late afternoon, she decided to wait until the next morning.

Chapter 9

Eloise was anxious to get home that night and call Joseph to see how the interview with the former police officer had gone. She and Sophia had been shopping downtown that day, and she thought about it several times while they were out. When she walked in the door and looked at her phone, she saw that the light was blinking, meaning she had a message—from her principal probably. She had not responded to his call about assignments the other day because she'd hoped to talk to one of the other English teachers to see if they had seen any problems. She didn't expect any, but just in case something had changed since last year, she wanted to talk with someone before she responded.

When she picked up the phone to get the voicemail, she heard Joseph's voice. "Eloise, could you give me a call when you get home? It's not exactly urgent, but I just need to talk to you."

And I need to talk to you, she thought. "How'd it go, talking to the former policeman? Was he any help?" she asked when he answered the call.

"Not a lot. I mean he was really a weird guy. Even Detective Barrett said he was weird. And at one point he got to asking me questions, almost like he was interrogating me. I was getting kind of nervous, and then Detective Barrett turned the questioning back around, but the guy even asked me what my sister's name was. I wasn't sure I should tell him, but I could hardly find a reason not to, so I did."

"So did you learn anything about the case that was helpful?"

"Not really. He kept saying they didn't tell him anything much, and no, he didn't see any reports, etc. It was just not at all what I expected."

"What did Detective Barrett think?"

"He said he thought the guy was weird too. In fact, he was the one that brought it up when we left. He said, 'Did that guy seem a little weird to you?' and when I said yes, he said that he just wanted to be sure he wasn't just imagining it or something like that."

"Well, it makes you wonder if he might be involved in some way, or know something he doesn't want to tell," said Eloise.

"I guess time will tell, but it makes me want to solve the case. I think we'd be doing my cousin an injustice by not trying to learn the truth. On another topic, are you still coming over next week?"

"That's my plan. Is it still okay with you?"

"Yes. I miss you."

"I miss you too."

"Could we go to a movie or something one night?" He asked. "I don't want us to spend all the time 'snooping.' I'd like for us to do something fun part of the time."

"I would love that," said Eloise. "Oh, and Rebecca said I could stay with her and Abby again. I talked to her yesterday."

"Very good. I'll see you next week then, and you can call me when you get to her house."

Eloise was feeling very good. Sophia had good news this week, too. She'd met a young man that lived close by that she really enjoyed talking to. He was an elementary teacher, as well, and he had many of the same ideas about teaching young children that she did. While Eloise was gone the week before, Sophia and this guy had gone out to eat and to a movie one night, and they had had a good time. His parents lived in Murfreesboro, but he had moved into Nashville after college, and he taught in the same school system that she did. They had made plans for her to meet his parents next week, and she was excited.

The next morning, she decided to call Mr. Chestnut, her principal, and find out about her assignments. She had not had time to call any of the other teachers, but she decided to call him anyway. The secretary said he was on another call, but she would have him call back when he finished. When he called, he sounded a little stressed. "This is Hugh Chestnut. Have you heard the news?" he asked.

"What news? I guess not." Eloise immediately became anxious.

"It looks like there's going to be some changes in the English Department this fall. For one thing, Mike is joining our administrative team. That means an opening in some slots. Then Ms. Miller has agreed to take a middle school position teaching seventh grade English. In addition to that, Ms. Jenkins has decided to retire, so that means there is an opening there. The big problem with Ms. Jenkins' slot is that we'll need someone to be the advisor to the yearbook staff. Things are changing every day, it seems. Would you consider working with the yearbook staff? I saw you'd had a little experience with that." It was the first time Eloise had felt that Mr. Chestnut had indicated that he really knew her, so she was honored that he would even consider having her take on advising the yearbook staff. At the same time, she was terrified of the responsibility.

"Oh, I'll have to think about that. I did work with the yearbook staff both in high school and in college, but I've never done it as an advisor. I remember thinking that it was a big job. To be honest, it kind of scares me. Can I give it a little thought? I know you're under pressure to get this all sorted out, so I'll try to let you know something tomorrow."

"Of course," said Mr. Chestnut. His voice was professional yet understanding. He had been principal there a long time, probably at least ten or fifteen years before Eloise had come, and she had not had many conversations with him. His white hair and movements indicated that he might be getting close to retirement. The very fact that he would notice her accomplishments made her want to do as he had requested.

As soon as she got off the phone with the principal, Eloise called Mrs. Jenkins. As she waited for an answer, she pictured the lady. Joyce Jenkins was a large woman by most standards. She wasn't exactly overweight, but she was significantly taller than Eloise and was rather big-boned. Her hair was turning gray, and there were a few wrinkles around her brown eyes. She looked rather tired all the time. Maybe she had some health issues, thought Eloise.

When she heard the familiar voice of her fellow teacher, Eloise said, "Joyce, this is Eloise. I just heard from the principal that you're retiring. First thing, 'congratulations!' I'm happy for you. And second, do you think I could handle being yearbook advisor? Mr. Chestnut seems to want me to, but I'm not so sure."

Mrs. Jenkins gave a little laugh. "I'm sure you can, and I'm not going anywhere. If you need me, I can give you some help. You were on the staff in both high school and college, weren't you?"

"Yes, and I enjoyed being on the staff in school, but I never thought about being the advisor. If you're willing to listen to me whine occasionally, I guess I can give it a try."

"Maybe we can get together sometime before school starts, and I can give you a few pointers," said Mrs. Jenkins. "And then you can think back to your own experience and what worked for you then. I think you'll be fine."

"It sounds like things will be all topsy turvy this fall. Did you know that in addition to you retiring, Ms. Miller is going to the middle school to teach, and Mike is going to be an assistant principal there at the high school?" Eloise asked her.

"I knew about Mike taking the assistant principal role, but I didn't know about Ms. Miller. That must have just happened last week."

"So, we have three vacancies to fill, and I'm not sure they've found any replacements at this point. Anyway, I think I'll give the yearbook advisor a try. It sounded like Mr. Chestnut was pretty stressed out, so I told him I'd let him know tomorrow. I'll try to be as cooperative as I can."

"I'm sure he'll appreciate that," said Mrs. Jenkins. "Did you know that he and I came here the same year? We both moved to Nashville from Memphis. We didn't know each other, of course. He'd been the principal of a middle school there, and I'd taught in a high school in the same area."

When she called him the next day, Mr. Chestnut seemed to appreciate her willingness to take on a new responsibility. "I was wondering if all the rest of the teachers in the department could come in one day and get together on what we need. That way I could find out if we have some applications that might fit what we need," he said.

"I think that's a good idea," Eloise agreed.

"I'll call all of them and set up a time. Probably early next week. I know that someone might be on vacation, but if so, we could get their input via email, or they could talk to one of the other teachers and give their input that way."

"Okay, I'll be out of town some next week, but I won't be leaving until Wednesday afternoon," said Eloise.

Mr. Chestnut said, "Let me check my calendar. What about Tuesday morning about 10:00? Would that work for you?"

"That would be perfect," said Eloise. "I'll put it on my calendar and see you then."

On Tuesday morning, Eloise was up and ready by 8:00. She had talked to Mrs. Jenkins about other classes she had taught last year to get an idea of what was going to be available and/or what would be needed. Mrs. Jenkins said last year she taught English IV. Eloise did not assume that she would be teaching any other courses that Mrs. Jenkins had taught, but it helped her to know. She had forgotten what Mike Johnson taught, but she thought Ms. Miller had been teaching ninth grade English. She looked through some of her folders that morning to see if she could find any of last year's schedules from the fall or spring semester but was unable to dig up any. She wasn't sure that would help much anyway, since enrollment varied each year.

Before long, it was time to go, and she drove off feeling some anxiety about what they would learn. When she arrived, she was received and led into the main conference room by the secretary. "He'll be right with you. He's gathering up some materials to help you decide what you'll need to plan for a good teaching staff this year," she said pleasantly. "He's really excited that you were willing to come in and help with this task."

Looking around the room, Eloise could not think of anyone in the Honors English department that was missing. With the loss of three teachers this summer, Eloise was glad that all the rest of the teachers were able to come. She had been teaching English III in the department for the last two years. Since she'd been asked to be the yearbook advisor, she hoped she'd continue teaching the same thing. If she had to change, it would be an additional challenge. She wondered if Mr. Chestnut would mention her new responsibility as yearbook advisor.

The first thing Mr. Chestnut did was give them a list of teachers who had applied, with a bit about each one to help them see possibilities to fill the vacancies. "Enrollment begins next week, so we don't have exact numbers, but it's usually not too different from the previous year. We know we need teachers for Honors English I, II, III, and IV anyway, so let's go over these applicants and see what you think. These four are already living in the area. I thought we'd look at them first. We do have a few from out of town if we need to look at them."

One by one the four applicants were discussed, and teachers made comments about how each might be good for each of the vacancies. Eventually, it was obvious to Mr. Chestnut which three stood above the rest. He said, "I think those three seem to stand out as good prospects, so why don't I call them in and let you talk to them? Meanwhile, I'll come up with some ideas about how the work could be divided. I heard someone commenting about Ms. Miller's English I classes being a good fit for one of the new applicants, maybe a first-year teacher. Another thing that has changed a bit is that Ms. Erickson has agreed to be the yearbook advisor. That's a big job, but now that Mrs. Jenkins is retiring, someone was needed, and fortunately Ms. Erickson was willing to do it."

"Thank you, Ms. Erickson," said one of the teachers. "I was wondering who would agree to do that."

"Well, I only have experience being on the staff in high school and college, not in being an advisor, but fortunately, Mrs. Jenkins has agreed to help orient me to that new duty. Let's hope I can do it sufficiently," said Eloise.

"Oh, you can do it," said two other teachers at the same time.

By the time she left, Eloise was feeling fairly confident, or at least thinking that she could probably handle it. Before they left, Mr. Chestnut had given them a date to come in and talk to the prospective new teachers. "What day did you say you had to go out of town?" he asked, looking at Eloise.

"Oh, I'm leaving tomorrow, but I will be back on Sunday, so I'll be here next week for the meeting," she said.

As they were leaving, one of the other teachers asked Eloise about her trip out of town. "Is everything okay?" she asked.

"Yes," she said. "I'm just involved with a murder investigation over in Hometown. That's all."

Of course, the other teacher wanted to know all about it, and by the time Eloise finished explaining, the teacher was even more curious. "It sounds to me like there might be something going on between you and that Joseph character. Am I right?"

"Well, maybe," said Eloise. "This is the first time I've felt anything for another guy since my divorce, so I'm being careful."

"Smart girl," said the other teacher. "I hope all goes well for you."

At the agreed upon time a few days later, the teachers were back in the conference room meeting the applicants they discussed that day. The first one was a man, John Freeman. John looked almost like Mike Johnson's opposite. He was short, a bit overweight, and a blond, curly-haired fellow.

Mike had joined them that morning, and it was his turn to ask the applicant some questions. Mike looked like a typical basketball coach—long and lean. He eased down into his chair, and asked Mr. Freeman his first question. "Do you like teenagers?"

When the guy answered in the affirmative, Mike smiled and said, "Then you'll be all right, man. That's basically all it takes. You have to like them. You will learn that most kids will do what you ask if they know you care about them and have their best interests at heart."

The other teachers began by asking him about his experience and then they told him what the vacancies were in the department, emphasizing the fact that none of them typically got exactly what they wished for, but they at least had some input. Despite looking like the exact opposite of the man he was replacing, when he left, they agreed that he was a good possibility for Mike's position.

Thirty minutes later, another teacher was ready to be interviewed and they hoped she would be a good candidate for Ms. Miller's ninth grade literature classes. Her name was Janice Day, and it was her first year of teaching. She was a wisp of a little woman, hardly big enough to be in high school, let alone teach there. She told them that she'd started the year last year in another school, but it didn't work out, and after the first six weeks she left. She was definitely not like Ms. Miller, who was always in charge, whether she was teaching freshmen or participating in a teacher's meeting. Her red hair made her stand out in a crowd, and she made a point of talking just a little louder than necessary to be sure her voice was heard. Janice seemed much more intimidated by the whole process than the other applicants, but that seemed normal for a first-year teacher.

They knew that Mrs. Jenkins' position might be a little more difficult to fill, but they interviewed the next applicant and found her to be a good possibility for one of the positions. At least it was a good start. When they talked to Mr. Chestnut, they told him what they had come up with, knowing that he might think otherwise.

Chapter 10

When Eloise saw Rebecca's number on the caller ID, she answered the call immediately. As soon as she heard Rebecca's voice, she could tell that something was wrong. "Are you okay," she asked her.

"Maybe I'm overreacting, but I just got a really weird phone call, and I wanted to tell you about it. I don't know who it was, but I wrote down the words he said to me, although I doubt that I'll forget them any time soon. These are his exact words: 'Rebecca, you need to tell Joseph to stop meddling with things no one can do anything about.'"

"Was that all he said?" asked Eloise.

"Yes. Then he just hung up. At first, I thought it was a woman, and then I decided it was probably a man. His voice sounded kind of whiny, not like anyone I'd heard before."

"Did you tell Joseph about it? What did he think?"

"I haven't told him yet. I decided to call you first. I don't want to make him stop investigating the murder. What do you think?" asked Rebecca.

"So this person actually called you by name and mentioned Joseph by name? That's really scary."

"It did kind of scare me, but what was I supposed to do?"

"I think you probably need to tell Joseph about the call," said Eloise. "In one of the newspaper articles we looked at the last time I was here, there was something about Charles getting harassing phone calls in the weeks leading up to his murder. That makes me wonder about you getting a phone call. Could the person be the same? I know it probably isn't after all these years, but it still makes me wonder."

"I guess you're right. Maybe I'll tell him when you're here," said Rebecca. "It makes me a little concerned that you and Joseph might be in danger, trying to investigate the murder. It's one thing for the police to investigate, but they have a bit of protection."

The following weekend, Eloise arrived at Rebecca's late Friday afternoon.

When Joseph came to pick her up, Rebecca said, "I need to tell you something before you all leave."

"Is it a secret, or can Eloise listen too?" asked Joseph.

"Oh, I've already told her, but yes, she can listen."

"Well, you two seem to be ganging up on me," he said.

"Not really," she said. "I just needed to talk to her about it before I bothered you with it," she said.

When Rebecca told Joseph about the phone call, he immediately said, "They called you by name? Well, yes, you did the right thing. I need to report that to Don Barrett. He'll know what to do."

When Eloise and Joseph left the house, she could tell that he was more upset about the phone call than he seemed back at Rebecca's. "I don't want to get Rebecca and Abby involved in this. I never thought about someone calling her. Do you think they could have been threatening her or trying to threaten me by calling her?"

"I don't know. Did you think about the fact that one of those newspaper articles talked about Charles getting harassing phone calls during the weeks before his murder?"

Joseph took a long breath. "No, I had not thought about that, but you're right. There was something about harassing phone calls to him. Was there any explanation about that in any of the materials we looked at down at the station?"

"I didn't see anything. We might ask Sergeant Jackson about it the next time we see him," she said.

"I just don't want to get someone hurt by looking into this," said Joseph. "Especially you. You be careful."

Joseph and Eloise went to dinner and went back to Rebecca's a little early. As they pulled into the driveway, Joseph said, "Let's plan to go back to the police station tomorrow morning and talk to Detective Barrett and Sergeant Jackson. I'd like to tell them about the phone call to Rebecca. I just don't like that."

When they got to the police station the next morning, Sergeant Jackson was not there, but they met with Detective Barrett anyway. When Joseph told him about the phone call that Rebecca got, he looked alarmed but sat a bit before he said anything. "Did she say anything about his voice? How it sounded? Was it distinguished in any way?"

"I don't think so. Did she say anything to you, Eloise?"

"The only thing she said about his voice was that she thought it was a woman at first, but later decided it was probably a man."

Detective Barrett sat and looked out the window for a bit, then turned to Joseph. "I think it may not be a good idea for you to continue digging into this case," he said. "First of all, I received permission to re-open the case, so I will have time allotted to work on it. In light of the call you got, it may be counterproductive to both of us for you to be asking questions about it. Why don't you just let us take care of it unless there's something I need you to do, which is unlikely. I don't want either one of you to get hurt in this. Okay?"

"I guess that goes for me too," said Eloise.

"Yes. It does. Maybe especially for you. You live in Nashville, don't you?"

"I do, and I teach school, so I'll be back in school soon. I doubt that I'll be a threat to anyone but just in case they think I am, I'll not be in town much."

As soon as they got back in the car, Joseph said, "You sounded like you'd be glad to be gone from here as soon as possible when Detective Barrett was talking. I hope you're not planning to dump me too."

"Not at all. I'm planning for you to spend more time in Nashville. How's that sound?"

"Better than not seeing you."

Both Joseph and Eloise felt the tension of their situation now. They had met and had been seeing each other mainly because of their mutual interest in the investigation of Charles Wright's murder that happened nearly thirty years ago. Now, they were told not to do any more investigating. Now they had a new motivation, not related to the murder in any way. How would they explain their plans now? They planned to go to a movie that night, and they had already shared that with Rebecca. Eloise wondered if Rebecca would expect her to go on back home the next day? Should she talk to Rebecca more about her feelings for Joseph? These questions were going through her mind as they drove back to Rebecca's after dinner that evening.

As soon as they got settled back in Rebecca's living room she asked, "Well, did you learn any more about the case today?"

Joseph looked at Eloise and then at Rebecca. "Well, not really. But I got thrown off the case, so I won't be working on it anymore."

"What?" asked Rebecca. "What do you mean? Did you do something wrong?"

"No, he didn't do anything wrong," said Eloise. "He just told the truth— as he should have."

"I felt like the detective needed to know about that phone call, and when I told him, he said that he had gotten permission to re-open the case, and we no longer needed to be asking around about it. It's all for the good."

Rebecca looked at him for a moment. "Well, now you two can just admit that all this time you've been spending together has not been just to work on the murder case. Now you can just be like any other couple who are dating." She laughed as they both blushed a little.

"Well, I guess I'll be sharing the traveling a little more. And more of our time together will be spent in Nashville," said Joseph with a smile as he looked at Eloise.

"Way to go, Brother," Rebecca said, and they all laughed. Joseph stayed a little longer that evening, and Eloise felt a little more relaxed.

The next day, Eloise drove over to Jane's and spent the morning with Jane and the boys. After having lunch there, she went back over to Rebecca's and spent the afternoon with Rebecca and Abby before Joseph came and got her for dinner and a movie.

As they drove back to Rebecca's that night, they took a little longer than usual to finish their conversations about everything. Their whole relationship had centered on the murder case, even though they both knew more was at stake. Now they just wanted to be together and share more about each other. They talked about their childhood, their youth, their hopes and dreams. Finally, they settled on a time for Joseph to visit her in Nashville. It would mean they wouldn't see each other for a whole month, but both of them knew that it would be difficult for her to take a whole weekend to be with him in Nashville the first couple of weeks after school started.

When he started back down the steps of Rebecca's front porch, she stood and watched him go, wishing he would come back up the steps and stay with her.

Rebecca welcomed her into the living room, where she had some fresh coffee and cookies for them while they discussed the day's events. Both of them were excited about the possibility of being "sisters" someday, but they were not bold enough to say it out loud.

"I hope I didn't upset Joseph too much by telling about the phone call," said Rebecca. "I felt like he needed to know about it though."

"Don't blame yourself. I could tell Joseph was upset thinking he had done something that might put you in harm's way, and he did the right thing by telling the detective. I also think the detective was somewhat suspicious of the way the former policeman acted. At least I was. I don't mean that I think the guy had anything to do with it, but he might actually know something he has been unwilling to tell. I don't know. Anyway, don't blame yourself.

I think the detective wanted to do it himself and not have any of us messing in it."

"I'm glad they are investigating again. It's not right for someone to be shot and killed and not find out who did it," said Rebecca.

They talked for a good while. Finally, it was time to go to bed in order for Eloise to get on the road early the next morning. She had told Joseph she'd call him when she got back to Nashville the next day. She told him that if things went as planned she'd probably be home by noon. She left on schedule the next morning but unfortunately, as she got closer to Chattanooga, the traffic was slowing down. The closer she got into the city, the slower it got. It almost came to a standstill, creeping along forever it seemed. One thing for sure, she wouldn't get to Nashville by noon. She'd be lucky if she got there by dinner time. By the time she got on to I-24 she was hungry and needing to go to the bathroom. At the next exit she got off for a bit of rest and realized that everyone else was doing the same.

When she finally got to Nashville, it was almost 4:00 p.m. in the afternoon, and she was exhausted. Knowing that Joseph had expected a call around noon, she called him before she unpacked her suitcase.

"Thank heaven!" he said when he heard her voice. "I thought you'd never call. Is everything all right?"

"Yes, but the traffic was horrendous," she said. She told him all about it, apologizing for the delay.

"Don't worry about that. Just get some rest. I'll call you tomorrow. By the way, when you have the chance, call Jane. She called me today to ask how things were going, but I didn't know for sure how much she knew about what had been going on, so I just told her that you were back in Nashville now, and I would have you call her."

"Okay. I'll call her tomorrow and explain the fact that the department is doing its own thing regarding Charles Wright's case. I'll also tell her that I may not be coming back as much, but that you and I will still get together. She'll probably be glad to hear that."

"Great. Love you, dear." It was the first time Eloise had heard those words from him, and they sounded right.

"Love you too," she said.

Monday morning, Mrs. Jenkins called her saying that she had talked to the editor of this year's yearbook, and that she was willing to meet with the new advisor sometime that week at Eloise's convenience—if Eloise wanted to that is. Eloise told Mrs. Jenkins that she'd definitely like to meet with her so they could "hit the ground running" when school started, and they came up with two different times during the week to offer the student, a senior who had been on the staff for three years. According to Mrs. Jenkins, the girl was very knowledgeable about every aspect of the yearbook production and would be very helpful. Eloise asked Mrs. Jenkins if she would be willing to meet with them.

"Oh, I would certainly be willing to meet with you and introduce you to her. Her name is Karen, and I just know you'll like her," said Mrs. Jenkins.

"I actually think I know who you're talking about," said Eloise. "I did not teach her in English III, but I was made aware of her at some point. I can't remember for sure, but I think she may have been in my class initially and then reassigned. "

She had agreed to meet with Mrs. Jenkins and Karen on Wednesday at 2:00 p.m. As soon as they got to the conference room and sat down, Eloise knew that Mrs. Jenkins was right. The sweet smile on Karen's face told her all she needed to know.

"This is Karen, Ms. Erickson, and she'll be your editor this year." The senior girl that had agreed to be the yearbook editor stood silently as Mrs. Jenkins introduced her and explained a little bit of what the role of the advisor is in helping students to produce a quality yearbook each year. Karen was a rather tall girl with long, straight blond hair.

"Great. You can probably teach me a lot about my job," said Eloise.

"I'm a little scared myself, to be honest," said Karen. "I'm used to having Mrs. Jenkins to keep me in line."

"Well, I guess we'll learn to figure it all out together," said Eloise. "My main concern is what needs to be done right away when school starts. Do you two know how many returning staff members we'll have—students that have some experience like you do?"

"I think I have a list somewhere of those who said they planned to come back," said Mrs. Jenkins. "I'll try to find it and pass it along to you in the next day or two."

"I know that the girl who was in charge of layouts last year is coming back," said Karen. "She is a good friend of mine, and I sort of begged her to come back because she was very good at her job!"

"Good for you!" Eloise said.

Mrs. Jenkins said, "In response to your other question, I know we usually get the business staff to start selling ads as soon as possible, but other than that, I'll look back at my notes from last year and give you a list of things we usually do at the beginning, but of course things change periodically so you will develop a schedule of your own, I'm sure."

By the time they left that day, Eloise was feeling much more confident, remembering her own experience as a yearbook staff member, including an editor as a senior both in high school and in college. When she told Karen about the two times she'd served as yearbook editor, Karen smiled broadly. "Oh my! I'm impressed. You can teach me a lot, Ms. Erickson. I didn't know any of this. I knew Mrs. Jenkins could teach me a lot, but now I know that you can too."

Thursday evening when her phone rang, she was hoping it was Joseph. She couldn't wait to tell him all about the meeting with Mrs. Jenkins and Karen. When she looked at the caller ID though, it was one she didn't recognize. "Hello," she said.

"I know you've been asking some questions about the Charles Wright murder," said the voice. *Man or woman? She wasn't sure.*

"Who is this?" she asked. Click. The caller hung up quickly.

Her heart was beating wildly. Who was this? It must have been the same person who called Rebecca. How did he/she get Eloise's phone number? It didn't sound like anyone she'd heard before, so she was pretty sure she had not given this person her number, and she was almost as sure that Joseph would not have given it out. He had been so upset about the person who called Rebecca and he was concerned about anyone who might be making a call like that. She spent the rest of the evening in turmoil. First, should she tell Rebecca or Joseph—or both? Probably both. And second, did this mean the person knew where she lived? She hoped not.

After thinking about it that evening, she decided to call Sophia Friday morning. When Eloise told her about the call the first thing Sophia said was, "Did the person threaten you or tell you not to ask questions or anything?"

"No," said Eloise. "That was all he said. It was like he just wanted me to know he had my name and number. I sort of felt threatened, but he didn't really threaten me directly."

"Well," said Sophia, "it sounds like the whole point was to make you *feel* threatened, so that you'd quit asking questions, and according to you, both you and Joseph have stopped having a part in the investigation, so maybe he'll stop bothering you."

"I certainly hope you're right. Do you think I should tell Joseph or the investigator about the call?"

"Well, it would seem that you are in no danger, but it might aid them in their investigation to know that those kinds of calls are being made. It certainly would not hurt anything to report it to the investigators, but in terms of protecting yourself, I doubt that it would be necessary," said Sophia.

"I feel the same way," said Eloise. "However, I really think Joseph would want me to tell him about it. He seemed pretty upset when Rebecca got that call the other day. I think I may call him tomorrow and tell him, just so he'll know if he hears anything, or if Rebecca should get another call."

Saturday morning, Eloise decided that she had to let Joseph know about the call she had gotten, so she called him that morning.

Joseph reacted just as she had predicted. "Oh, no. Eloise! I am so sorry. I wonder how he got your number. I certainly didn't give it to anyone."

"I know you didn't, Joseph. Probably someone gave it to a person they trusted, and it got into the wrong hands. But anyway, I don't want you to feel responsible in any way. I was just wondering if Detective Barrett needs to know about it. What do you think?"

"I think he needs to know. Especially since Rebecca got a call also. Like you said, your number and Rebecca's were probably given out in complete innocence, but they may have given it to someone who is a 'friend of a friend' or something like that."

"I know. I was thinking of the many times I've talked to people and someone in the group needs a phone number. Usually someone else will say, 'I'll bet so and so has her number.' There's just no way to know how phone numbers get shared. Should I call him, or do you want to do it?"

"I can call him, but he might want to talk to you also. If he does, he has your number."

"Okay. That's great. With school starting, I've got a lot going on."

"How's it going? Are you feeling okay with the new assignments?"

"Oh yes, it's all okay, just busy."

"Is it still okay if I come next weekend?"

"Sure. I'm not *that* busy. Will you get here in time for us to go to dinner, or will I just need to have a dessert ready?" she asked, laughing as she spoke.

"My plan is to leave work early and be there in time for us to go to dinner. If it doesn't work out, I'll call you when I leave. How's that?"

"Perfect," said Eloise. "Oh, one more thing about the phone call that you may want to tell Detective Barrett. You remember that Rebecca said at first she thought it was a woman, but later decided it was a man? It must have been the same person, because I felt the same way. I thought it was a woman at first but then decided it was most likely a man."

"I'll be sure to tell him that," said Joseph. "I'm really looking forward to next weekend."

"Me too," said Eloise.

Chapter 11

By the end of the week, things were looking good at school. The teachers had been working all week, and Eloise was feeling good about her classes of English III. She'd met several of her students because they had come by after they finished registration. Also, Karen, the yearbook editor, had dropped by one afternoon to visit and tell her about other staff members she'd talked to that morning. She said that almost all last year's staff would be returning except those who graduated. Eloise was glad to hear that, because it meant that although she was new in her position, most of the staff would be experienced, and that would make it easy to have leaders who were familiar with their jobs.

Leaving work Thursday, Eloise was feeling really optimistic and excited, and before she got home, she decided to run by the grocery store that was close to her apartment and pick up the ingredients to make a cake for her and Joseph this weekend. After all, he could be late Friday evening and they could have it then, or they could just have it over the weekend, depending on when they wanted it. She was sure she could remember everything she needed to make it since she had made it often over the years. It was her favorite, so she was sure Joseph would like it too.

Twenty minutes later she was on her way to the apartment. As she entered the kitchen with her hands full of groceries, her phone rang. She put everything on the table and answered without even checking the caller ID.

"Hello," she said.

"I'm thinking you are in regular contact with your mother," the voice on the other end said. "If so, tell her that she may have gotten out of town before she was found years ago, but now we'll be able to find her and make sure she keeps her mouth shut. Also, if she's told you anything, you'd better keep yours shut too." Before she could speak, the caller hung up.

Eloise sat down. She was shaking uncontrollably. It was the same voice she'd heard before. Obviously, the caller was not aware of her mother's death. She could not think beyond that. She was overwhelmed with grief–for her mother, for herself, for Charles Wright, for everything she'd learned that she knew had burdened her mother for years. Her mother had left a place she'd loved to protect her daughter but never spoke a word about it. Finally, she stood and put away the groceries. When she gained a little more control of herself, she decided to get busy making the cake as she had planned.

Friday began with a brief meeting with the other Honors English teachers, including the three new teachers. Two were seasoned teachers who had moved in from another state, and one was just out of college. She had attended Belmont in Nashville, so she was reasonably familiar with the area, but she seemed a little overwhelmed with the schedule and the workload for the fall. Eloise tried to reassure her that she could come to some of the other teachers if she needed help. Since Friday was the last day before they would have students on campus, there wasn't much time to calm her down. Eloise wished she'd talked to her a little earlier in the week, but it was too late to worry about that now. Maybe it was just last-minute jitters, and she'd be fine come Monday morning. Of course, Eloise knew there was little she could do because she would be entertaining Joseph all weekend. She left with mixed feelings, hoping that the new teacher would be okay.

As it turned out, Joseph arrived that evening in time for them to go to dinner, which made Eloise happy. She had planned to go to a steak restaurant, knowing that he loved steaks. If he wanted to go to a movie afterward, there was a theater nearby that had seven or eight different movies to choose from. Two of them were movies she knew he would like. She decided not to mention the second phone call until after dinner and the movie. When she mentioned going to a movie after dinner, however, he said he'd rather go to a movie on Saturday evening. "I'm more interested in just being with you tonight," he said.

"That suits me," she said. "In fact, I wanted to be with you too. I had a scary experience last evening that kind of freaked me out."

"What happened? Don't tell me you got another phone call!"

"Actually, I did. I don't know what to make of it. I think it was the same person who called before. And obviously the caller did not know that my mother had died. But the call was more threatening than the last one. And it appeared that Mom had left because either she'd been threatened or she thought she was in danger. Of course, she never told me anything about why she left."

"I remember that you did not even know that Charles had died before you and your mother left, so it makes sense that she could have known something that made her want to leave. What exactly did he say?"

Eloise relayed the caller's message word for word to Joseph, and told him that the call was a little more threatening, mainly to her mother but also to her if she knew anything.

"Did he say anything that led you to believe he has any idea where you are?"

"No, and my cell phone doesn't really have the area code that most Nashville residents have, so he might not think to look that up. If he did, then he'd know that it's close by, but since I live in downtown Nashville, he'd still be at a loss on how to find me."

"I wonder if he knows that you're a high school teacher."

"I doubt it, unless the person who gave him the number knows, which is possible I guess."

"This is just bizarre. Let's talk about something else," said Joseph. "For now, at least."

"Sounds like a good idea to me. We're just making me scared."

After dinner they went back to her apartment and had some cake for dessert and watched a little television for a while. Saturday, they toured Nashville a little and then went to a movie that evening. By Sunday, Eloise was getting used to having Joseph with her when he brought up the phone call again. "Do you think it might be better for us to be careful where we spend time together in the future until they get this investigation finished? I can't keep from thinking someone could be tracking us trying to find out where you live or something."

"I was wondering about that too, but the thing is, this is an old case, so no telling how long they'll have to investigate."

"That's true. I guess we should not meet back in Hometown, but I will keep checking in with the detective, and maybe ask him if he thinks we should find some other town to get together in for now."

Eloise smiled. "I know a good place to meet if we wanted to meet in another town," she said. "I have a friend in Knoxville. She has a little cabin over in East Tennessee. I think she'd let us stay there for nothing if we needed to for the weekend once in a while."

"That sounds perfect to me. I'll ask Barrett if he thinks we are in any danger by meeting in Nashville. He'll probably think we're fine, but if he says it would be safer not to meet here, that sounds like a viable option."

Late Sunday, Joseph and Eloise said their goodbyes, and he headed back home. Their discussions about the phone calls she had received left a bit of worry with Eloise, but she tried not to think about it. She did tell Sophia about the recent call and updated her on all she and Joseph had discussed about their plans.

When Joseph got back to Hometown, he immediately called her. "I hope I didn't upset you too much," he said. "I got to thinking about it when I was driving home. I shouldn't have mentioned anything about there being any danger. There probably is none. After all these years, any guy that would have been involved back then is obviously a lot older now. He might be able to make threatening phone calls, but probably not inclined to go after someone who lives out of town without a lot of help. Please just try to ignore all that. I will tell Barrett about it, but I don't think you need to worry about any of it."

"Thank you, but please don't worry about me. I'll be fine."

Chapter 12

On Monday morning, Eloise was more concerned about meeting with her students than any worries about some hypothetical threat. The new English I teacher was entering the building as Eloise was getting out of her car. Since she'd parked close to the building, Eloise waved at her to wait, and they walked in together. Eloise noticed that Janice looked like she might have been crying.

"Are you all right this morning?" she asked her.

"I guess," Janice said. "I just hope I can do this. I tried last year, but I just couldn't do it."

"Oh, you'll be able to do it this year," said Eloise. "We'll all help you."

"I hope so," said Janice. "Last year, the teachers all seemed to be so critical. I know I don't have as much experience, but how can I get experience unless I get a little help to get me started? They always pointed out my faults, which I'm sure were many, but it didn't help me to be reminded of what I was doing wrong all the time."

"You're right, Janice. Just think about the kids and try to figure out what they need. You may have more in common with them than some of the older teachers."

"I hadn't thought of it that way," said Janice.

Eloise had a busy day, with no time to think about how poor Janice was doing, so at the end of the day she was surprised to see her in the hall showing two young freshman girls where the library was located. She heard both girls saying, "Thank you, Ms. Day. See you tomorrow."

Janice walked down the hall toward the office with a smile on her face when she saw Eloise. "Looks like you've made it through the first day with flying colors," said Eloise.

"Indeed, I have," said Janice. "Your encouraging words this morning were so helpful."

"You know that if you need anything to get through these first days, you can always call on me. I'm just two doors down the hall from you," Eloise told her.

"That helps," said Janice. "I hope I won't need anything, but it's comforting to know you're close by."

About that time, John Freeman came out of the office. He greeted Janice and Eloise. "How was your day?" he asked.

Both Eloise and Janice said they had a good day. "And you?" asked Eloise.

"Best first day I've had in a long time," he said. "Everyone here is so friendly and helpful. And so far, my students have behaved themselves well."

"You'll find that to be generally true," said Eloise. "I'm not saying they're perfect by any means, but I've not had much trouble with students here."

Eloise had taught English III for the last two years, so she was beginning to feel comfortable doing that. The yearbook staff, however, was a little more difficult. She had worked with Karen last week to settle on some possible deadlines, but she still had to confirm them with the principal and office staff. Both Karen and Mrs. Jenkins had mentioned that the staff always confirmed deadlines with the administration before announcing them. Mrs. Jenkins said that they had to be careful to avoid other deadlines and plans which might cause them to be unable to meet their deadlines. When that happened, the yearbook staff usually felt the heat about it. When she'd asked Mrs. Jenkins about assignments, she said sometimes students came in with their own ideas about what they wanted to do, and other times she'd just ask them to take on a task that needed to be done. She said that often the more artistic students liked to do the layouts, and those that liked to write wanted to work with the copy. On the other hand, it all had to be done, so that meant that often those that chose to work with layouts had to do copy also, and those who loved to write would sometimes have to create layouts. Karen seemed to be able to do any of it adequately and was willing to do anything that needed to be done. On the other hand, she was a little reluctant to make assignments to the other students. Sometimes Eloise would find her working very hard to get something done that she should probably have assigned to someone else.

Those that chose to be photographers had to be reminded that it was important that they be responsible and not waste time. Also, they had to divide up the after-school assignments so that just one or two didn't end up having a very heavy load.

All students were required to sell ads and turn in their money and plans to the business manager on time. That responsibility was completed early in the semester, and then those students were allowed (or required) to become part of either the copywriting and editing team or the layout team.

Eloise kept in close touch with Mrs. Jenkins, calling her regularly almost every week to get some tips on how to manage some of the tasks that had to be done.

After the first two weeks, Eloise was feeling good about Janice. She had not sensed that anything was going wrong for her. Then one day at lunch, Janice had approached her and asked, "Could I come see you after school today?"

"Sure," said Eloise. "Just come on to my room when school is out."

All afternoon she wondered what Janice needed, telling herself that everything was probably fine. Janice entered the room a few minutes after the end of school. "Hey, how was today?" Eloise asked.

Janice sat down at a desk near the door and put her head down on the desk. Eloise wasn't sure if she was crying or just tired. She waited a few moments and then asked, "Is there anything I can do to help you?"

Janice lifted her head. "I just don't know if I can do this or not! There's just so much to do and the students don't seem to like me."

Eloise sat quietly for a bit, collecting her thoughts. "What makes you think students don't like you?" she asked.

Janice began, "Oh they sometimes argue with me, and often look at me like I don't know what I'm talking about. And . . . I don't know."

"Could you tell me a little about what happened last year? I think you said you tried to teach last year and had to quit."

"Well, I didn't get fired, but I was afraid I was going to. I was just so scared."

"Did you do something you weren't supposed to do, or something that they didn't like?"

"I don't know, but this afternoon, I started feeling a lot like I did last year. Just scared that I couldn't do it."

"Did you get any help? Like going to a counselor or anything?" asked Eloise.

"No, I just decided I couldn't do it."

"But this fall you came back to teaching—so you seem to like some things about the profession, don't you?"

"Oh yes, I like lots of things about it. I guess there's just some things that a person can't do, even if they like to do it."

Eloise walked over and placed her hand on Janice's shoulder. "I don't know about that, Janice. Have you ever been treated for panic attacks? Or have you ever thought about that you might be having a panic attack?"

"What's that? I don't know."

"I can't explain all about it to you, but I know there is such a thing and just wondered if you'd ever thought about getting some help dealing with these feelings. Sometimes people give up on something they really want to do because it's difficult when they might be able to overcome the problem."

"I had never thought about getting help with it. I just thought I couldn't do it," said Janice. She raised her head and looked at Eloise.

Eloise said, "Would you be willing to talk about this with our counselor? She might know someone who could help you work through your anxiety about the job instead of giving up."

"Yes, I would be glad to talk to her if you think it's a good idea. I just don't know what to do. I think 'panic' is a perfect word for the way I was feeling when I came in here today."

"Lots of people have what they call 'panic attacks' but I don't know much about it. I certainly can't diagnose anyone. I just know that some people go on medication to help with it. I also know of people who have talked to a therapist to learn how to deal with the feelings."

"Would you walk down to the counselor's office with me? I don't think I can go alone."

"Of course I will. I think she will know more about what might help, and I know that she knows a lot of other counselors and their specialties."

Eloise and Janice walked together to the counselor's office, where the counselor was finishing a conversation with the principal. As he left, Eloise introduced Janice to the counselor and asked if she had a moment to speak with them. "Sure," said the counselor, who had worked at the school ever since Eloise had been there. After Eloise briefly explained what she'd told Janice, she felt like Janice was eager to explain more to the counselor. She left the two of them and headed out the door. She didn't want to prevent Janice from confiding in the counselor.

Two weeks later, Janice came to Eloise's room after school to thank her for putting her in touch with the counselor, saying that not only had Eloise been right about her problem, but that the counselor had found another therapist that was helping her immensely. At this point, the therapist she was seeing had not thought medication was necessary but was considering that as an option should she need it. "I am feeling so much better though, and I'm giving you all the credit. No matter how long I teach school, I will always remember your help during a time when I was about to give up on myself and my ability to teach."

Eloise could tell that Janice was improving over the next few weeks. It showed in her face and the pace of her walk. She talked with Janice regularly and could tell she was gaining ground. She was enjoying teaching, and her students liked what she did.

One day when she got home from school, she had a message from Joseph saying he had some important news and needed her to call him. As soon as she got the message, she dialed his number. When he answered, she said, "What's the news?"

She heard him laugh as he said, "Boy, that was quick. I only left the message a few minutes ago. Maybe it's not the sort of thing you're thinking. They haven't caught the killer or anything, but I may have found out how your number got out. Jane called me the other day to find out how the investigation was going, and as we talked, I mentioned the calls you'd received. And then I said something like, 'Who would have given her number out? I didn't, and I asked Rebecca and she had not given it to anyone. It's just a big mystery.'"

"Jane was quiet for a moment and then she said, 'You know it may have been me. Of course, I didn't give it to anyone who would have made those calls, but I did give it to a friend a few weeks ago. She could have given it to someone, not knowing whose hands it would get into.' It turns out she gave it to this friend because she wanted the friend to get to know you because she thought your mother and hers had been friends at one time. Anyway, she said she didn't know the woman too well, and she could have mentioned it to some friend of hers, who gave the number out to someone else. You know how that goes. I just wanted you to know that."

Eloise said, "Well, I suspected something like that. I hope Jane doesn't feel too bad about it though."

"I told her not to worry. If she hadn't given it out, someone else might have anyway. Who knows?"

"Maybe I should call her and reassure her that no one is blaming her."

That weekend, Eloise decided to call Jane. As soon as she realized who it was, Jane started to apologize for giving out the phone number. Before she could go further, Eloise said, "Jane, you did nothing wrong. Any of us could have done that. I'm certainly not blaming you. There's no way you could have known the number would get in the wrong hands."

"When Joseph told me that someone called you and made you feel threatened, I was so upset. I just knew you'd hate me for it."

"Jane, you know that you didn't even have to tell him that. It's not your fault. Of course, I was upset when I got the call, but it made me even more determined to find Charles' killer."

Jane said, "Excuse me just a minute." Eloise could hear her speaking to the boys. "Ben, stop that. You might cause him to fall. Get down. Now." When she turned back to the phone, she said, "I'm sorry, Eloise. These boys are getting worse every day." She laughed. "I know they're just boys, but I get so frustrated with them sometimes."

"I think you're just being a good mother, Jane. I know it's hard sometimes, but they're going to grow up to be fine young men,"

"I hope so," said Jane. "Tell me about the school year. How's that going?"

"So far it's been good," said Eloise. "We have one first-year teacher and she has struggled some, but I think she's on the right path now."

"I'm sure you've been a big help to her. Joseph said you were advising the yearbook staff this year. Is that working out all right?"

"Yes, it is. I had never done that before, and as Joseph might have told you, I was a little nervous about it. But I didn't realize how familiar everything would be since I'd actually worked on the staff both in high school and in college. Of course, I had a different role then, but knowing most of the parts of the job helped me to be able to think of ways to guide them through the tasks of putting the book together. I have a great group of students on the staff, and the editor is very sharp. Her only weakness is that she is reluctant to delegate to the other students. Her tendency is to just do it herself. I'm working with her on that, though. I think she's getting better too."

"I can imagine she'll learn a lot from you," said Jane.

'I hope so. That's what I'm there for."

"Oh, I also wanted to ask you about the murder case you and Joseph were looking into. I was disappointed to learn that you are no longer involved in the investigation, but I guess it's all for the good," said Jane. "When I first learned about it, the only thing I could think was that you might not be coming over here anymore."

"After the threatening call to Rebecca, I think Joseph and I were both glad that Detective Barrett had received permission to re-open the case.

I know they can get the job done quicker and more efficiently than we could. We spent all our time trying to decide what to do next." They both laughed.

"When Joseph said you'd gotten a call too, that was scary. And then when he mentioned that 'someone' had given out your number, I panicked. But I had to let him know that I'd given your number to a friend. I still hope nothing bad will come of it."

"I don't know that you've heard about this, but I actually got a second call that was a little more scary than the first. It sounded like the caller didn't know that my mother had died, so he was talking about whether she'd told me anything. He seemed to think that she might know something about the killing of Charles Wright."

"I can't imagine how my friend would have given the name to someone who would do something like that." Jane was obviously disturbed about giving out the phone number, but Eloise was sure she had not intended any harm when she did it.

"She probably didn't do it intentionally. Try not to worry. I know you meant no harm, and she probably didn't either. Joseph has reported the whole thing to the detective, and they'll work on it for us."

"When you talk to Joseph again, please tell him that I'll be glad to tell the police the name of the person I gave your number to, or I can call her and see who all might have it now," said Jane.

"No need for you to call anyone yet. They might not want us asking questions at this point, but I will mention it to Joseph," said Eloise.

After the call, Eloise was relieved, but she was sorry Jane was so upset to think she'd been the cause of her friend getting a threatening call.

Chapter 13

Eloise and Joseph kept in close contact, but were unable to get together as often as they would like. They did go up to the Knoxville area one weekend, but they were a little afraid that someone might find out, so they felt like they were, as Joseph put it, "sneaking around."

"I want everyone to know we're a couple. In fact, I want to marry you," he said one evening while they were in Knoxville. "But we can't until they get this stupid investigation finished."

"I know," Eloise said. "Have you heard anything lately?"

"Not really, but I think they may be making progress. The last time I went by to see Detective Barrett, he made some comment about thinking that he might be closer to making an arrest than I thought."

"I hope you're right," said Eloise. "Nothing would please me more than to be done with this."

"Are you saying yes to my weird proposal?" he asked.

"I guess I am. Did I hear something about wanting to marry me?" As Joseph nodded his head, she said, "Then the answer is yes!"

"Then I guess I'd better give you this," he said, pulling out a ring box from his coat pocket.

They both started laughing. He put the ring on her finger and gave her a long kiss. "I never thought I'd propose like this to anyone, but I'm glad you're going along with it,"

"Well, at least I can share it with my fellow teachers at school," she said. "They may believe I'm just making up this person I'm engaged to, but at least I have the ring."

Although most of their communication was by phone, Joseph made one visit just before Christmas. He left town heading toward Knoxville in case anyone was watching. When he got to Knoxville, he instead turned west toward Nashville. From what the detective said, he didn't think anyone would actually follow him all the way to Nashville. Except for the phone calls, he said there was no other indication that Joseph was being monitored in any way. After Christmas, Joseph had settled back into his work, and Eloise had gone back to school, accepting the fact that they could not visit as they wished. They talked on the phone, and Eloise had told him all about her friends' reaction to her mysterious fiancé.

The months of January and February came and went with no word from the detective, but on March 1, Joseph got a call from him. "I just want you to know that we've made an arrest in the Charles Wright case. In fact, we've made two arrests. You and Eloise don't have to worry anymore. You will get no more threatening phone calls. She will be perfectly safe if she wants to come into town. If you all want to come into the office together, I can give you both the whole story, or you can come in alone. Since we have confessions from both, we're only dealing with the judge's sentencing and they'll both be in jail until then."

Joseph called Eloise immediately. "Guess what? You can come to see me anytime you want to now. They've arrested Charles' killer, and there's no danger in you coming to town."

"What? Are you kidding me? We're free to celebrate our engagement?"

"That's what detective Barrett says," he answered.

"That's the best news I've had in a long time," said Eloise.

"My next question is, can you come to town this weekend? If so, we can go together and get all the details—that is if you want to know all the details,"

"Of course, I want to know," she said. "In fact, since it's already Wednesday, I might just come Friday morning, so we can go sometime Friday afternoon. I need a day off anyway. I haven't had one this year I don't think."

"Great, I'm sure you can stay with Rebecca, but I'll check to be sure. I need to call her anyway."

"Tell her I'll just need to stay Friday and Saturday nights. I'll have to come back here on Sunday and get back to school on Monday," said Eloise. "Oh, I'm so excited to know they've finally caught the culprit on this decades-long mystery."

Eloise got on the phone immediately and called Sophia to share her news. Sophia already knew about her engagement, and she knew how stressful it had been for both Eloise and Joseph to be engaged and not be able to share it in his hometown. They talked for a long time that evening.

The next morning, she told Mr. Chestnut as soon as she got to school that she needed to be off on Friday and would need a substitute. He looked at her in a funny way and said, "Are you okay, Ms. Erickson?"

"Oh, yes, I just need to go out of town early, but I'm fine."

He smiled at her. "I'm sorry. I don't think you've been absent this year, and I guess I was surprised."

Eloise had not shared much about the investigation with anyone at school yet. She had told a few people when she'd gone over to Hometown for the weekend, but she'd say she was going to visit a friend or something like that. After it was all over, she would probably explain everything to some of her friends, but so far, she had not. She realized now that she felt she was not in danger of any kind that this year had been rather stressful. She had not even admitted to herself that she'd lived in fear for several months because of the phone calls.

When she saw Janice that morning, she told her that she would not be at school the next day. Like the principal, the first thing Janice asked was, "You're not sick, are you?"

"No, I'm fine, but I'm going out of town for the weekend, so I decided to leave in the morning. The traffic is better that way. I'll also have a little more time there."

"Have a great weekend," said Janice. She seemed much more relaxed and confident than she had at the beginning of the year. It made Eloise smile as she left Janice's room that morning.

She informed each of her classes that they'd have a sub the next day and gave them a brief preview of what they'd be doing. She assured them that if they had problems with the assignment, she'd help them on Monday. When she met with the yearbook staff, she made sure each of them knew what they needed to do the next day.

She and Sophia had decided last night to go out to dinner on Thursday evening. While they were eating, Eloise shared with Sophia how relieved she was to learn that there would be no more phone calls since the case had been solved. "I never realized how fearful I was until I learned that I wouldn't have to worry about it any more."

"I think I know how you feel," said Sophia. "My mother and I always feared that my father would find us when we were living in California. She'd always tell me not to stray far from our home when I was little, and then as I got older, she still thought there were certain places he might show up. I didn't understand it so much when I was little, but as she revealed more, I began to be fearful also. Sometimes I still am, but I think the longer I live here, the less I think about it."

"Were your younger sisters aware of your mother's fears? Did she tell them not to go certain places too?" asked Eloise.

"I don't think they were aware as much as I was. Being the oldest, I was the one Mother talked to the most, and I never said much to my sisters. When we were little, I'd just say, 'Let's stay and play right here,' if they started to go further than I knew Mother wanted us to go."

"Is your mother still fearful?"

"I think by the time we moved here, she was beginning to be less afraid."

"You told me about why you came to the U.S., but I never thought about how your mother must have been constantly afraid he'd come and find you."

"Fear can paralyze you in many ways," said Sophia. "My mother showed her strength by getting us away from the abuse, but it still influenced her all the time. I think she's conquered most of it now though. She's managed to get us all through college now, and she recently got a new job managing a little store down close to where she lives. One of the churches helped her get scholarships for each of us, and jobs that helped us with other expenses. Each of her accomplishments gave her strength."

"She's an inspiration to everyone, isn't she?" asked Eloise.

"She certainly has been to me," said Sophia. "I could never have made it without her. I hope I can show her how much she has meant to me as she grows older."

When Eloise left Sophia that evening, she realized the strength it had taken her own mother to leave her hometown and come to a new place with a preschooler, probably afraid for her own life and the life of her daughter. Until recently, she had not realized that about her mother. It made her thankful that they had finally solved the case of the murder of Charles Wright, even if it was after her mother's death. She looked forward to hearing the details that had been hidden for so long. She wondered just what communication her mother had with anyone in Hometown. She had no family there. Her husband left long ago. Her mother and dad lived in Ohio, but both were deceased before all that happened. She probably just left and never looked back. Eloise hoped that she was not fearful of someone finding her. Of course, technology has improved a lot since the mid-eighties. Whatever had happened, Eloise realized that their mothers must have had some things in common. She wished they had been able to spend some time together. They had met a few times the year that Sophia moved to Nashville and become friends with Eloise, but after the girls started driving, the mothers never had much opportunity to get together.

She packed a few things before going to bed that night, knowing that she wanted to leave early the next morning.

Friday morning, Eloise left according to plan, thinking that she'd missed most of the early morning work traffic and could be in Hometown in time for lunch. Joseph said he'd told Barrett they would like to see him around 2 p.m. As she drove that morning, Eloise kept wondering who had actually been arrested, what the motive was, and what the real story was. Of course, they were most likely people she'd never met, but what if she had met them? Joseph's friend Spencer, for example–what if he'd been involved, or knew more than he shared? She decided it was not a good idea to get suspicious of every person she'd met, so she decided to think about her wedding. Soon they would need to decide where it should be and when. They could even make some decisions this weekend.

The time difference meant that she got there a little later than she'd thought she would, so she went straight to Joseph's office. Spencer was in the front office when she entered and expressed surprise to see her. "Wow, it's been a while since we've seen you here! But it's good, of course. Joseph is in his office, I think. Does he know you're coming?"

"He knows I'm coming, but I didn't specifically say I'd come to the office or what time I might get here," said Eloise, as she headed down the hall toward his office. She knocked lightly on the door and was pleased to hear his voice say, "Come on in."

When she entered, he immediately jumped up from his desk and walked toward her as she closed the door behind her. When he enveloped her in his arms, all the tension she'd had the last few months seemed to melt away. "You will never know how relieved I am to be at this point in time," she said.

"Me too," he said. "I tried not to worry, but I'll have to admit it wouldn't go away completely."

"I sort of miscalculated, not thinking about the time difference and all. I hope we'll have time to get lunch before our meeting with the detective."

"Yes, we'll be fine. I thought we'd get a bite to eat at the deli near the police station. That way we'll save some time and won't have to worry about traffic or construction work. How does that sound?"

"Sounds great to me," she said.

She left her car there and rode with Joseph. When they arrived at the deli, it was not too full and some of the customers were leaving. They could tell that it would not be a long wait. "I'm thankful it's not too crowded at this time," said Joseph. "Sometimes it's a bit of a wait, but I thought that the main crowd from around here might be finished and gone by now, and it looks like I was right."

"Did he tell you any names of the people who were arrested?" asked Eloise.

"No, I think I told you word for word what he told me, and I didn't ask anything once he said we could come together to learn exactly what happened."

An hour later, they were ushered into a conference room where both Sergeant Jackson and Detective Barrett were already sitting at the table.

"First of all, I want to thank the two of you for your continued interest in this case," said Sergeant Jackson. "We don't always tell people the whole story about a cold case like this, but we feel like it would never have been solved without your persistence, and that you need to know exactly what happened. In one sense, we believe it was a failure on the part of the police department that caused the case to go cold. Of course, none of us were here at the time, but still. . . " He hesitated at that time. "Anyway, our first break came when Joseph and Don went to visit a former policeman who was working here at the time Charles Wright was murdered. I'll let him tell you about that."

Joseph sat up at that. He remembered that both he and Don had mentioned how Philip had acted weird during the interview, but he didn't remember much about what was said. Don looked at Joseph. "I didn't tell you at the time because it was such a big revelation. It wasn't what he said, but his voice that struck me."

Don went on to tell them about his memory of the night Charles Wright was killed. It was the first Friday night after he'd broken up with his girlfriend and he had not planned to go to the basketball game, but he decided to go after all. "I was very perplexed at what I remembered so clearly about that night. As soon as we started talking to Philip, I was transported back. I didn't tell you because it pointed straight at the killer, and yet I'd never thought of him as being involved or being a violent man. I finally decided that I had to tell Sergeant Jackson."

"The first thing we did," said Sergeant Jackson, "was to talk to Rebecca, Joseph's sister, about what the voice that called her sounded like. When we talked to her, we were convinced it was Philip who made the call."

"After that, we asked Philip to come in to talk to us. At first, he was reluctant to comply, but when we reminded him that if he wouldn't, we'd get a warrant, he agreed to come in. We began by telling him that we had it from a good source that he was the one who made the threatening phone calls to both Rebecca and Eloise," said Don.

Sergeant Jackson then said, "In the meantime, we asked about people who were around and had any knowledge about the case, and an older lady came in and told us a few details that she knew about. It mainly had to do with the nurse who worked for Charles Wright. This lady was friends with the nurse at the time. The nurse told her that one of our policemen had given her some pills to help with Charles Wright's aunt. His aunt was in a lot of pain, and the nurse had used the pills to help alleviate the pain. After the nurse's death, this woman was a little suspicious of the policeman because he was at her house when she got hurt and later died. She didn't know if it had anything to do with Charles' death, but she wanted us to know about it."

"Did the lady say it was this Philip who had given the nurse the pills?" asked Joseph. "I remember him making some comment about thinking the nurse was a drug-user or something when we talked to him."

"Yes, the lady gave us his name," said the sergeant. "However, even if she hadn't, we would have known, because only one person at a time in the department has access to drugs that have been confiscated, and we had the records that listed him as having access."

"By the time Philip was brought in, we had all this to confront him with. There were still several questions to be answered, however. We already knew that he was with the nurse the night she was injured, but no one was accused of trying to kill her, and even if she was hit with something that caused her to fall and hit her head, why was Charles killed, and who was the person with Philip that night?"

Eloise asked, "Did you remember anything about this other person when you remembered about Philip?"

"No. Apparently I didn't know him, or I was just so struck by the voice that I remembered so clearly that I didn't pay attention to him. I could hear Philip's voice as if it were yesterday, but once I ducked out of sight, I couldn't see them anymore. And it was a brief comment from Philip that I remembered anyway. I don't remember any comment from the other person. I just knew someone was with him. But Philip's voice was the key. Even after all these years, I can still hear him saying, 'We don't have to worry about him anymore.' As soon as Rebecca and Eloise both described the voice on the phone, I knew it had to be him."

Sergeant Jackson continued, "We confronted him with what we had. At first, he kept saying that he had nothing to do with the nurse's or Charles' deaths, and he didn't know anyone that did. Finally, I told him we had confirmed that he was with both victims when they were injured, as well as when Charles was killed, and that if he couldn't give us an explanation for what happened to them, he'd be charged in one or both their deaths."

"After that," said Don, "he began to cooperate. After vowing that he didn't kill either one, he began to explain what happened. He admitted that he pushed Marie, the nurse. He had been in a relationship with her at the time he'd given her the pills. Soon afterward, they had broken up. Then he got worried that she might have told someone. On the night of her 'accident,' he said he had gone to her apartment to ask her if she'd told anyone that he'd given her the pills, and she was not sure. They got into an argument, and he pushed her. She fell against the door jam and passed out. He called the EMTs immediately, but she later died in the hospital."

"So, why wasn't he arrested then?" asked Eloise. "Did the police know that he'd pushed her?"

"I doubt it. Some of it was public, of course, but I doubt they knew that he'd pushed her and why. Later, he got to thinking that she might have told Charles. This is where the other guy comes in. This man was a long-time friend of Philip's from back in high school and had been in trouble with the law time and time again. Philip told him that he was concerned that Charles could cause him to lose his job if he knew about the pills. According to Philip, his friend said, 'I can help you—I can make sure he doesn't do that to you. We'll go over there, and you just let me work my magic on him.' Philip said the guy was a charmer and he could usually talk people into doing almost anything, so Philiip thought he was going to either threaten him or promise him something that would make him not tell anyone. But when they got into the house, the guy didn't even talk to Charles much. He made a few disparaging remarks to him and walked over to a bookcase behind where Charles was standing and the next thing he knew, the guy was firing shots at the man's head. Philip said, 'I was scared stiff. We walked out of the house, and that was it.'"

"Did Philip admit saying 'Guess we won't have to worry about him anymore'?" asked Joseph.

"He said he was so scared that he didn't know what he'd said. He said that was the last time he'd seen the guy. He thought he'd left town that night or the day after. Apparently, the guy has been living below the radar ever since. That's one thing that took us so long to find the other guy. When we finally found him, he was in jail in Georgia. He has since been transferred back to Tennessee. He confessed when he was brought back. He had already been sentenced to thirty years for something for some crime in Georgia."

"Did you ask Philip whether he asked my mother if she knew anything or not?" asked Eloise.

"Oh, yes, I did. He did say that your mother 'got away' and that he always thought she may have known about the pills Marie had got from him. He seemed shocked when he learned that your mother never even told you that Charles had died, and that she was killed in a car accident a few years ago."

"So, where is the case now? Will Philip have to spend time in prison?" asked Joseph.

"I don't think that's been decided yet, but he probably will. It's still being decided what penalties will be assigned to both those guys. I'm sure that was the reason Philip made those calls when he learned that the case had been reopened. But one way or another, in my opinion, they'll both spend some time in prison. It just takes time to figure it all out." When Sergeant Jackson finished, he and Detective Barrett told Eloise and Joseph that they appreciated their getting the process started by digging into the case. "It might never have been solved without the two of you and your insistence that the case should be re-opened."

Joseph and Eloise left with a lot on their minds. Neither of them said anything for a few minutes, and then Joseph said, "Well, dear, we've got a wedding to plan."

"Yes, and I'm ready to start something new and positive."

"My next question is, when and where?" said Joseph.

"Let's go to Rebecca's and talk with her about it. I may need her help."

Chapter 14

Rebecca was waiting for them when they finally got to her house. There was a striking resemblance between her and Joseph. When Eloise saw one of them, she immediately thought of the other. At the same time, there was a difference. It was like they were two parts of one person. Rebecca was the feminine half and Joseph the male. They had definitely inherited many of the same genes. The warmth of their smiles and their voices made both of them attract many friends. Both Rebecca and Abby ushered them onto the porch for a report on what they'd learned.

After they finished sharing all about what the policemen had told them, Abby said, "I want to see the engagement ring!"

Eloise held out her left hand. "And I want to show it to you!"

"Oh, you did good, Uncle Joseph," said Abby.

"Yes, he did," Eloise said. "Joseph and I need to talk to you about a date and place for the wedding."

Rebecca said, "I assume you're looking for a venue in Nashville?"

"No, I was thinking about having it here instead of in Nashville. There are a few friends I'd like to invite from there, but it seems, I don't know, right to have it here where I began my life. And I think my mother would like that."

"That's wonderful. I could certainly be more helpful to you if you had it here," said Rebecca.

"Don't you do a little wedding planning?" asked Eloise.

"I do. It's been mostly for my friends. I don't advertise myself as a wedding planner or anything, but I'd be glad to do what I can for you."

"She's really better than she lets on like she is," said Abby. "At the last wedding she planned, one of my friends said that when she gets old enough to get married, she wants Mom to do her wedding."

"Maybe I'll be good enough by then," she said, smiling.

"Well, that's good enough for me. I won't be having a big wedding, so it shouldn't be too hard. I'll probably just have my friend Sophia as my Maid of Honor and maybe one other person. I might invite a few of my teacher friends, but I don't know if any of them will come. And you all and Jane and her family are the only people I can think of to invite. I'm sure you have some others you want to invite, Joseph, but I don't really know anyone else."

"We could probably have the wedding at my church, if you wanted to," said Joseph. "It's small, but we could just tell them they're welcome to come if they'd like. Most of the friends I have here go there anyway."

"Hey, that's not a bad idea," said Rebecca. "I've helped with several weddings there, and the ladies there will be glad to help with the reception afterward. They usually ask what we want for food at the reception, and they order it for us."

"I like that idea too. That way I could get to know a few of your friends, too," said Eloise, looking at Joseph.

"Now let's talk about a date. Do either of you have something coming up that you know would be a conflict?"

"I guess we'll have to do it during the summer months," said Eloise. "Maybe July. June might be too early, since I don't get out of school until the end of May. My Maid of Honor is also on the same school schedule."

"Okay," said Rebecca. "I'll check with the church and see what they have available during July, and you ask your friend Sophia if she has any conflicting weekends in July. Were you thinking Saturday or Sunday?"

"Probably Saturday. What do you think, Joseph?"

"Yes, I think Saturday is best, but I guess we could have it on Sunday. Let's start with Saturday, and if there's a problem, we'll talk about it."

Rebecca was looking at her notes. "What about music? Do either of you have some kind of instrument, song, or a soloist you'd like to have at the wedding or at the reception?"

"Didn't you sing a solo at someone's wedding recently, Abby?" asked Joseph.

"Yes, but Eloise might want something different than that," Abby said shyly.

"No, I won't," said Eloise. "Whatever you sing, that's what I like."

It turned out that the song Abby had sung was one of Eloise's favorites.

"I hope that we've not just taken over your wedding," said Rebecca. "Please feel free to add your ideas or nix some of ours at any time."

"Oh no. I'm very happy that you're willing to help," said Eloise. "I don't know much about weddings."

"One more thing. Do you want me to ask the pastor to do the ceremony and the vows, and print an order of service for the wedding, or did you have someone else in mind you'd like to ask to perform the ceremony?"

"No, I mean yes to getting the pastor to do it. I'd forgotten all about that. It's a good thing you know what you're doing, because as you can see, I don't have a clue."

Since it was getting late for dinner, Rebecca decided to order a pizza for them, and Joseph stayed through dinner. It had been a long day, and they were all tired. Joseph told Eloise he'd pick her up at 11:30 a.m. and they'd go to lunch together.

At lunch the next day, as they were eating, Joseph said, "Eloise, do you want me to use my influence to find you a job here, or am I going to have to find a job in Nashville?"

"I was thinking the same thing. What do you want?"

"Well, I'm happy here, so I thought I'd see what you thought we should do. If you really want to stay in Nashville, I'd give it a try, but I do kind of like being close to Rebecca and Abby."

"I like being near Rebecca and Abby too. In fact, one of the thoughts I had the first time I met Rebecca was that she seemed like family. I do want a job, of course. I wondered if you might be able to introduce me to some of the possibilities here in town. Even if nothing opens this fall, I might get a chance later in the year. Why don't you ask around this spring and see what you can learn. I won't turn my notice in until a little later, so that I might know what I'll be doing before I resign."

That afternoon they drove around town. There were two high schools in the area. One was with the system that Joseph worked for, which they both preferred. The other one was also a possibility. The schools were about the same size, but the one attached to the system Joseph worked for was a county system and the other was with the city. Before Joseph took her back to Rebecca's that evening, he asked her if she'd like to visit the church with him the next day. She said she would.

Before they went to bed that evening, Eloise asked Rebecca why she and Joseph went to different churches. "Well, I'm not sure. I think at the time I married, my new husband wanted to go to a different church from my parents, so we joined the one Abby and I belong to now. I've thought about going back to the church Joseph goes to but just never got around to it. Both Abby and I have so many friends where we are. I may just wait until Abby is in college. I think it would be hard to change right now. In a small town like this everyone knows everybody else and sometimes it's easier to just stay put. Both the churches are good, so there are no theological problems with either of them."

Before he picked her up Sunday morning, Joseph called Eloise to say that one of his friends had asked him if he and Eloise could have lunch with him and his wife after church. "Can we do that with your schedule? I know you'll need to leave in time to get back to Nashville before it is too late."

"I think that will be fine. I hoped I could meet some of your friends before the wedding. I had not planned to leave until mid-afternoon anyway. After all, I have to eat lunch somewhere. It'll give Rebecca a break to not have to feed me," she said as Rebecca passed by her chair on her way to the kitchen.

When she finished talking to Joseph, Rebecca asked, "I assume that was Joseph. What was he planning for your lunch?"

"One of his friends had asked us to go to lunch with him and his wife. He didn't give me a name for the couple, since I wouldn't have known them anyway. Who do you think it was?"

"Probably Sam and Amy," said Rebecca. "I don't know for sure, but Joseph and Sam are good friends. They play golf a lot together. I don't know Amy as well, but she's a high school counselor, so you'd probably get along well with her."

Eloise was glad to visit the church where she would have the wedding. She noticed so many things that reminded her of the church she and her mother had gone to occasionally when she was younger. This church was a bit smaller, but the service was very similar in many ways. After the service ended, Joseph introduced her to the pastor and his wife, telling them that Rebecca would be contacting him about doing their wedding during the summer. "That's fantastic," said the pastor. "I'm so happy to hear that you want to have the wedding here."

Sam and Amy were waiting for them outside, and Sam suggested that Eloise and Joseph ride with them to the restaurant. "That way we can visit a little more," said Amy.

"Okay, that sounds like a good plan," said Joseph.

When they got in the car, Sam said to Eloise, "Did Joseph tell you that we've known each other ever since I moved here?"

"No, he didn't. How did you meet?" asked Eloise.

"Well, at the time we were both teaching high school social studies, and I was coaching basketball. Some kid got us mixed up and asked me a question which he should have asked him. Do you remember that, Joseph?"

"Yes, I do, because we laughed about it for a long time and teased him about it."

When they got out of the car at the restaurant, Amy said to Eloise, "Do you plan to live here after the wedding, and if so, might you teach at one of the high schools here?"

"I'd like to do so, but of course I don't know yet. Joseph plans to see what might be available in the county system for me. Rebecca said you are a counselor in the city system. I'd appreciate it if you'd keep that in mind in your school as well."

"I will certainly be glad to do it," said Amy.

"Eloise, just so you know, I've asked Sam to be my Best Man for the wedding," said Joseph. "I forgot to tell you last night."

The restaurant was crowded, typical for Sunday lunch, according to Amy. Fortunately, though, they were soon seated. The waitresses were pleasant and brought their food in a timely manner. "This place is wonderful," Eloise said, as she lifted a piece of fried chicken off her plate. "When I get here, we'll have to eat here every Sunday!" They all laughed, glad they'd chosen a place she liked.

They all got to know each other a little, and soon they were on their way back to the church to retrieve Joseph's car. On the way back to Rebecca's, knowing that Eloise would have to leave soon, Joseph said, "I don't know that I've ever been this happy. I can't wait to be married and have you here all the time. But since that will be a few months, when will you be able to return to finish wedding plans?"

Eloise took out her calendar. "I would like to come near the end of April. And then I can come at the end of May and stay until the wedding. How does that sound?"

"Perfect. You'll need to come to my place and figure out how to make it your home, or we can move to a new location if you don't like the idea of living there," said Joseph. "In fact, if you have time, we can run by there now, and you can look around a little. It's just a short distance from Rebecca's. I think you've only been there once, and you probably weren't thinking about living there then," he said, laughing.

"You're right. I just barely remember being there. I think it was right after I met you."

Joseph's house was quite similar to Rebecca's, but the decorations were very different—everything looked "manly" to Eloise. "Yes, I may need to think about some changes, but I think we should just stay here. I like the location and the basic features of the house. I might want to change a few of the decorations, though," she said, smiling at him.

"I have no problem with that," he said. "I want you to feel like it's ours, not mine. Why don't you start with one room, just think about what you'd like to change in that one room first and go from there—or the kitchen or bedroom, whatever you see that you'd like to improve a little."

Eloise turned around and threw her arms around him. "How did I ever have the luck to find a man like you? Thank you for being you!"

They looked around a little more, and then Eloise said, "I really don't want to leave, but I'd better get back to Rebecca's and prepare to go back to Nashville. I want to get a good night's rest before tomorrow. We've got so much done this weekend and I'm so thankful for it."

"We have, haven't we? We've made so many decisions so quickly. I hope you don't get back to Nashville and regret any of them. If you do have doubts about anything, just call me and we'll change it. I just want us to be together. That's the main thing for me."

They walked to the car and Joseph drove her back to Rebecca's, walked her to the door and gave her a kiss. "Okay, you two lovebirds, it's parting time—and I did not say 'partying' time." Rebecca was standing in the door-way watching them with a big smile on her face.

After Joseph left, Eloise told Rebecca how pleased she was with all they had accomplished during the weekend.

"I'm proud of both of you," said Rebecca. "I've never seen Joseph so happy. He's been a little down during the time when he could not see you as often and he was worried about the phone calls you'd received. When that detective called and told him they'd arrested both those men, he just perked up dramatically, and then when you said you wanted to come this weekend, it was like daylight had come over him. I'm so happy for both of you."

"This has been the best weekend," said Eloise. "I think being able to come back here has done me so much good."

"How did you enjoy the church service?" asked Rebecca. "And what did you think of Sam and Amy?"

"I loved the church. It reminded me of the church Mom and I attended some in Nashville. It is a bit smaller, but it seemed similar in many ways. Joseph introduced me to the pastor. He was so friendly, and it made me glad we had decided to do the wedding there. We went to that restaurant not too far on down the road—I can't remember the name of it."

"Oh, Carley's I bet."

"Yes, I think that was it. Lots of people there, but the workers were up to the task. And I really like Sam and Amy, too. I think Amy and I will be good friends."

"I'm glad you enjoyed it. I thought you would, and I figured you and Amy would have a lot in common. I've known Sam for a long time, and Amy just seems so sweet."

"After lunch, Joseph and I went by his house. I'd forgotten what it was like, but I think it's great, so we will just stay there after the wedding. He said I could do some redecorating, and I probably will, but it's not bad the way it is."

"You may want to make it a little more feminine," said Rebecca, smiling.

"He said he'd move to Nashville if I wanted him to, but I like this town. I'm sure I can find a teaching job at some point. I'd even take a middle school position for a while If I had to."

"I'm glad you want to move here. He told me that he'd move if he needed to. I was sure hoping you'd want to come here, but you would have been within your right to insist that he be the one to move. I sure am glad you want to live here, though. It's not just because I want my brother here. I like having you around. And Abby loves you. She's thinking of all kinds of ways she will enjoy having you as a relative and friend," said Rebecca. "She keeps referring to you as her 'soon-to-be' aunt."

As Eloise drove back home, she realized it was the first time since her mother died that she'd been truly happy. Not only was she happy about her upcoming marriage, but there was something about Rebecca and Abby, as well as Jane and her family, that felt like home to her. It was getting close to dark when she got back to her apartment that evening. She decided to wait until the next afternoon to call Sophia.

Chapter 15

Although Eloise had been engaged for several weeks, this weekend made the idea so much more real to her. She began to think more about what it would be like to move from Nashville to the little town she'd left as a small child. As she thought about the prospect of moving back, she began to think about what it must have felt like for her mother when she left the safety of that little town and moved to the big city. Although her mother had not talked much about working at the insurance agency, Eloise remembered a little bit about loving the coziness of the little room her mother worked in and the safety she felt when she was in the office building. When she and Joseph had driven out to his house, they passed by the office. She didn't mention it to Joseph, and she wondered if he was even aware that Charles had once owned it. It had a new name now. She wasn't sure that it even looked the same on the outside, but she remembered sitting on the floor beside her mother's desk, while her mother gave her paper and crayons to color with until her mother finished work. There was something about going back to the little town and getting married and living there that was appealing to Eloise. Somehow it made her feel closer to her mother. As she drifted off to sleep, she felt safe and ready to begin a new life with Joseph.

The next morning Eloise woke up with her mind a jumble of thoughts. Everything she'd learned about what happened to Charles Wright, of course, was on her mind as she drove to school. But her own future was on her mind, as well, including the fact that she realized she only had a couple of months before school was out, and she would not be seeing her students or her fellow teachers in the fall. She also wondered how Sophia would feel about Eloise leaving Nashville. Since Sophia knew about the engagement, she would probably not really be surprised that Eloise would be leaving. The same would be true of her fellow teachers, but the reality of it all was just now sinking in. Everything was happening so fast.

When she got to school, the first thing she did was head down to Janice's room to check on her. She was pleased to find her steady and confident, as she had been for several weeks. "How was your trip?" Janice asked.

"It was fine. I've got lots to tell you, but it'll have to wait until this afternoon, I guess. Did everything go all right Friday without me?" Eloise asked.

"The best I could tell It did. Your substitute seemed very capable. She's probably one of the more experienced ones."

"Well, I'll go on down to my room and get ready for the day. I had a very busy weekend, so I don't have too much energy today, but I'll make it."

Her students had just finished *The Grapes of Wrath* and were doing some research on some of the issues dealt with in the book. She had left some reading material for them to learn more about their chosen research topics, but she'd also suggested that they look at several websites on the internet to find more material. She was pleased when some of the students came in and told her what they had found. Some of them even told her they'd gone to the public library over the weekend and found additional material they could use.

"I never knew anything about the Dust Bowl history," said one student. "That was fascinating—and also sad for many people."

"It's amazing how much they leave out in American History books," said another student. "I never saw anything about that period of history. They seem to just focus on the wars."

"That's true, but there's a lot more to life than war and politics," Eloise told them.

There's one thing Eloise learned that day—the school could function without her. She ended up telling a couple of her friends that day that she and Joseph were getting married during the summer, and that she would be moving away and would not be teaching there in the fall. She asked them not to mention it until she was able to tell the principal that she would not be returning.

As soon as she got home that day, she called Sophia. "How would you like to be my Maid of Honor in my wedding this summer?" she asked.

"I'd love to, but what do I do? And when is the wedding?" Sophia asked.

"Well, we hope it can be held on a weekend in July, and to be honest, I have no idea what the Maid of Honor does. But my wedding planner knows, and she's going to be my sister-in-law! How cool is that?"

"That's perfect for me and you both," said Sophia.

"So, can you be in my wedding any Saturday in July?" asked Eloise.

"I have nothing on my schedule. I am at your service, girl. And I want to know all about your weekend," said Sophia.

"Oh, Sophia, there is so much to tell. Every minute was special. I'm afraid it's too much to share in one setting. We'll have to have a sleepover or go out for a long dinner or something."

"You name it," said Sophia.

"Okay, I will tell you a little about the murder case. Do you remember me telling you about Joseph going with the detective to interview that former police officer?"

"Yes. I do remember that."

"Well, it turns out that he was the one who made the calls to both Rebecca and me. And he was present at Charles' death. It's a long story, and I'll tell you more later, but he'll be in jail for a while."

"Oh my gosh! Did you have any idea?"

"No, but you see I never really met him. It was a very entangled story that I had no idea about. And that was just Friday afternoon. It was a long weekend. But fortunately, the rest of the weekend was much more pleasant. Why don't you come over tomorrow after school, and we'll visit, go to dinner, and I'll tell you more about what happened and what the future looks like."

"Like I said, I'm all yours," said Sophia.

That night, Joseph called Eloise just as she was getting ready for bed to tell her that they could have the wedding any Saturday in July as far as the pastor could see. "I just need to know which Saturday suits you and your Maid of Honor the best."

"Fortunately, for me and for you, Sophia says she can come any Saturday of the month. I was thinking I'd like to have it on the second weekend. Has Rebecca expressed a preference?"

"You're not going to believe this! She said the exact same thing—the second Saturday it is!"

"She and I think a lot alike."

"True," said Joseph. "I've thought that for a while. I'll pass the word along to the pastor and to Rebecca and Abby about the date. Is there anything else I need to tell Rebecca?"

"No. I may call her later this week. Also, tell her to feel free to call me any evening if she needs anything. I want to talk to her a little about sending a few invitations, and I also need to talk to her about the reception."

"Okay, I'll tell her. Does that go for me too—that I can call you any evening?" he asked.

"Of course. You know you can. By the way, some of my teacher friends have been asking if they will get to meet you, so I told them you might come over one weekend before school is out. Do you think we can work that out?"

"I think so," said Joseph. "Look at your calendar and I'll look at mine. The next time we talk, we'll work it out. I guess I'd better go now, but I'll talk to you in a few days."

When Eloise visited Joseph in April, she and Rebecca spent most of the weekend working on a list of people who would need to receive an invitation. They were mostly people Eloise worked with in Nashville, along with Sophia's family and a few of Joseph's friends who lived out of town.

Joseph was coming up the first weekend in May to meet some of her friends, so she spent the week planning how to best structure the weekend. Sophia was helpful, suggesting that she and her boyfriend would plan to take them on a tour of Nashville on Saturday and include another couple that Eloise taught school with. Eloise decided to invite the rest of the teachers, along with Sophia and her boyfriend, to come over to her apartment on Saturday evening for desserts and snacks. She thought that would be more relaxed and allow them to visit more than trying to go somewhere and eat a meal. She and Joseph ate a late lunch and planned to have snacks for dinner.

Not all of Eloise's friends were able to come, but Joseph got to meet several of her coworkers, and he seemed to enjoy that. It was nearly midnight before they all left, and both Joseph and Eloise were tired. Before he left the next day, Joseph gave Eloise a big hug and thanked her for planning a special weekend for him. "I'll be much more comfortable when they show up at the wedding, now that I know them," he said.

The closer it got to the end of school, the more Eloise worried that there would not be a job opening for her in Hometown. She had not actually resigned from Hillbrook, but several teachers knew that she was getting married in July. She needed to let them know since she would be sending out invitations. She entertained the idea of staying on staff at Hillbrook the next year, or at least in the fall, but Joseph hated the idea. He said they could probably make do on his salary for a while if she was not hired in the fall. They both thought the added burden of her living in Nashville and traveling back and forth might be almost as much of a financial burden as her not having a job. She was beginning to feel panicky about the situation.

Here it was the beginning of May, and she still hadn't heard anything for sure about a job. Joseph called her one evening. After talking about it for a bit, he said, "Eloise, I think you should just turn in your resignation. I'd rather take on a part-time job somewhere for a few months than have you traveling between here and Nashville every week or so. Also, being here would be an advantage because you could start immediately if something came up. Don't you think so?"

"You're right. I'd feel much better to just get this behind me. And if I need to, I can take a job teaching in one of the middle schools for a while."

The next morning, the first thing she did when she got to school was to go in and talk to her principal. "I need to tell you something," she began.

"Oh?" he said. He was looking at a folder in his hand.

"I'm getting married in July, and I won't be returning this fall," she said.

"I sort of suspected something might be going on with you," he said. "Well, congratulations! But we'll miss you around here. You've been a blessing to our school." He seemed genuinely sorry she was leaving but was gracious and wished her well. That was one more load off her mind. She realized that with each decision she made, she was transitioning to her next challenge.

The closer it got to the end of school, the more Eloise realized that she'd need to dispose of several items before she left for good. Her landlord had agreed that she could leave a few things in the apartment, because he was not planning to rent it again until the fall. He said he wanted to paint the kitchen and bedroom during the summer, and for her to leave anything she wanted to come back for in the living room, where it wouldn't be in the way of the painters.

After telling the principal, the next time she met with the yearbook staff, she felt that she needed to tell them. She called them together. "Before we get started today, I need to make an announcement to all of you," she began.

"What did we do wrong?" asked one of the layout staff members.

"Oh, it's not about what you're working on," she said. "It's about my plans. I'm getting married this summer, and I'll be moving away, so you'll have a new advisor this fall. I just wanted you to know that I've enjoyed working with you this year, and I'll miss you. I'm sorry that I only got to work with you for one year. I didn't know my plans when I accepted this assignment last fall."

"Oh, we'll miss you too, Ms. Erickson," said one of the girls.

Karen looked at the girl that had agreed to be editor next year. "Oh honey, I'm sorry. I really thought Ms. Erickson would be the advisor again. I know you'll do a good job though, even with a new advisor, because I was in your shoes last year. And guess what? I got a good one. You'll do fine," she said, as the future editor looked like she might burst into tears.

"Of course, she'll do fine," said Eloise. "No matter who the new advisor is, she'll be lucky to have you at the helm."

After their conversation, the staff gradually retreated back to their tasks. Although several students asked Eloise about her plans, not a lot was said after that day about the fact that she would be leaving at the end of the year.

After she'd talked to the yearbook staff, there was one more person she wanted to have a good talk with, and that was Janice. Eloise remembered the first time she saw her at school. She was an extremely thin little thing, smaller than most of the ninth graders she taught. Had she been more observant, Eloise might have noticed how ill-at-ease she seemed and may have predicted the panic attacks that came on her early in the school year. She was so pleased with the progress Janice had made as a first-year teacher, and she hated to leave without being reassured that the young teacher would be okay.

The last week of school, Eloise invited Janice to go to the little coffee shop near the school and visit for a while. Janice knew that she was engaged, but they'd never really talked about her plans to leave Nashville. She thought Janice might have heard about it from someone else, but she wanted to talk to Janice personally.

When they got to the coffee shop, Janice looked at Eloise and said, "I have a feeling you're going to give me some bad news."

"Well, it's not bad news from my standpoint, but I did want you to hear it from me. My wedding will be in July, and I'll be living in the little town where my fiancé lives after that, so I won't be teaching here next year. Had you already heard it from some of the others?"

"Not exactly, but yesterday, I overheard two of the students talking, and one of them said, 'I knew she was getting married, but I didn't know she would not be here next year.' Somehow, I knew they were talking about you. I don't know why, but I did."

"One reason I wanted to talk to you today is because you will be getting an invitation to the wedding any day now, and I wanted all the teachers to know in case they wanted to come together. It will be on a Saturday afternoon, so it would be feasible to drive over just for the day."

"I don't know too many of the teachers well enough to ask them for a ride, but I would love to come, especially if it were only that day."

"We'll keep in touch. I'll try to call you in a couple of weeks and tell you of any who are definitely coming."

"You've made my first year a success story, and I really appreciate it," said Janice. "When I came here last fall, I was so fearful. I had failed at my first year of teaching, and I guess I expected to fail again. But here I am now at the end of my first full year of teaching, and I'm already looking forward to the fall. Now isn't that something?"

"It sure is," said Eloise. "I'll look forward to hearing all about it too. My problem right now is that I haven't found a job there. Or should I say Joseph hasn't found me one. He works for the superintendent's office, so he has access to any resignations they'll get from English teachers."

"I'm sure they'll be getting some any day now, and they'd sure be lucky to get you," said Janice.

"You're sweet to say that, but I am getting a little panicky now. Maybe something will turn up, though. I'll miss you and all my friends here, but I'm excited about living there. The town is friendly, and Joseph's sister Rebecca will be a big help to me."

When the two teachers finished their coffee and left the little shop, Eloise felt much better about the prospects that her friend would do fine this fall, whether or not she was there to help her.

The last week of school, while Eloise was dealing with finals and getting all the yearbooks sold, she and Sophia spent each evening packing things that she was taking with her the next week. Joseph had taken several things back with him when he was in Nashville a few weeks earlier, promising to not unpack them until Eloise got there to decide where to put them. Mostly he took winter clothes and a few small things like two small tables she'd bought at an estate sale last year, and some bedding she wouldn't need.

Sophia wanted Eloise to go with her over to visit her mother and sisters before she left. They planned to go on Saturday after school was out, since Eloise had decided not to leave until Sunday. Sophia's sisters didn't live with their mother, but they had agreed to be there so they could visit with Eloise before she moved. One of her sisters was a nurse and one was a sales representative for an insurance company. Gabriela, Sophia's mother, worked with the preschool at her church. They had planned to meet at Sophia's mother's house around 11:00 a.m., visit a while, and then go to lunch at a cafeteria down the road from where Gabriela lived.

The minute they arrived at Sophia's mother's, her mother ran out to meet them, and after giving Sophia a hug, she hugged Eloise, telling her how happy she was for her. "But I don't know how Sophia and I will do without you, dear, because you're one of the first people I remember meeting when we moved here, and except for a brief period of time during your college years, you've always been around. You are just like my fourth daughter. I'm going to miss you so much."

"And I will miss you—my second mother!" Eloise said. Gabriela kept her arm around Eloise as they approached the steps to the porch and into the house.

Eloise relished Gabriela's hugs. It felt just like a hug from her own mother. She was always so affectionate with both Sophia and her sisters, but she also made Eloise feel loved. She was short and a little overweight, but not enough to be considered obese. Since her own mother died, Gabriela had filled the gap when she needed it. It was sad to realize that she might not see her much after this.

They talked a little more, but before long Maria and Ana were there and they were all talking at once it seemed. Soon after, they headed down to have lunch. Eloise enjoyed every minute. They were just like family to her. Before she and Sophia left, Eloise turned to Gabriela.

"Are you still planning to come to the wedding?" she asked.

"Yes, but Ana can't come because she has to work," said Sophia's mother. "At first, she thought she'd be able to get off, but one of the nurses had an accident last week, so they're short-staffed for the next month or so, and the hospital needs her. But Ed and Sophia will be coming of course, and Maria and I will be there too."

"Great. The Hampton Inn is holding a number of discounted rooms for out-of-town guests. Just let me know if there are any problems. I think I put that information in all of your invitations."

"Yes. It was in ours. We've talked about it and Maria or Sophia will be making our reservations in the next few days. We were waiting to be sure about whether Ana could come."

Later, as they were driving back Eloise said, "Are you and Ed serious?"

"I think so, but I'm not too sure. I get the feeling that some of his family may be concerned because I'm Mexican," she said.

"Do you mean his immediate family, or just some extended family?"

"I think maybe a cousin, but I'm not sure."

Eloise looked at her for a moment. "Ed should not pay attention to them. If he does, it's his loss, not yours."

"I think he's a good person," said Sophia. "I've watched him with kids at school. He's so kind to all of them, no matter what color or nationality they are. He may just have to figure out how to deal with a few of his relatives. Or I guess he may be trying to decide whether he wants to get married or not."

"Maybe our wedding will inspire him," said Eloise.

"I hope so," said Sophia.

"Does your mother like Ed?" asked Eloise.

"Oh yes, she loves him," said Sophia. "And Ed's mother loves me. There's not a problem between our immediate families. My sisters love Ed, too. He's so good to them."

"That's a real blessing. My problem is I have no siblings, but Joseph's sister Rebecca is really good to me. I don't know if I could have this wedding over there without her. She and her daughter are precious, and they feel just like family to me—from the day I met them."

When Eloise got back to her apartment that night, she felt grateful for her friend Sophia and the many ways they had experienced friendship over the last several years.

Everything was packed and ready for travel by Sunday afternoon when Eloise got a phone call from Joseph. She had told him that she would call him when she left, so she was surprised when she saw the caller ID on her phone. Her first thought was that he must have expected her to leave earlier. When she answered, the first thing she said was, "I know I'm slow today, but I'm almost ready to leave."

"No, no you're fine, but guess what? You have a job at McDougal High School teaching English III if you want it. I just got a call from a buddy of mine who is the principal, and he confirmed it—even on a Sunday. You can contact him sometime this week."

"Wow! What perfect timing. That's wonderful. I guess it was just meant to be."

"Will you be in town in time for us to go to dinner this evening? They've opened a new Outback Steakhouse recently, and I thought we could try it tonight if you want to," said Joseph.

"Sure. That will be fine. I should be there in plenty of time. I need to bring some stuff over to your house, so you can tell Rebecca I'll see her around eight or nine tonight, if that's okay with her schedule."

"Will do. You be careful driving then."

"I plan to," said Eloise. "See you in three or four hours."

Chapter 16

When she pulled into Joseph's driveway and parked her car, Joseph was coming out the front door before she could get out of her car. She was weary from driving, and after a good hug from Joseph, they began to bring in some of the things she wanted to leave with him. As she looked around the living room, she couldn't believe how spacious it seemed. Compared to her small apartment in Nashville, it seemed like a mansion. At the same time, it also felt comfortable. Suddenly, she realized she felt at home there.

"This already feels like home," she said. "I may not need to do much 'renovation' after I move in."

"You'll probably feel differently after the wedding," Joseph responded with a sly smile.

When everything was put away, Eloise sat down in the living room, and she said, "Now tell me all about my new job. I'm so excited."

"Well, the other day Randy, who is the principal over at McDougal, called me and said he'd heard that we were getting married, and that you might be interested in a job teaching high school English. Of course, I told him that was true. He said he'd like to talk to you. He told me that one of his teachers had just called and resigned a week after their school was out. So, I told him you'd call him when you got in town, and then I called you."

"It sounds like just what I wanted, doesn't it?" said Eloise.

"It does, but I don't want you to feel obligated. If it doesn't seem right when you talk to him, don't take it."

"I won't, but I think it'll at least be something I'll want to try."

"You said the principal was a friend. Who is he?"

"I went to college with Randy. He and I have kept up since then. I think you'll like him. He has several years' experience, and McDougal is one of the county schools my superintendent serves, so I keep up with it regularly."

"About how many students do they have enrolled in the school? Do you have an idea?" asked Eloise.

"I think it's somewhere around 2,200 but I'm not actually sure. I know it's one of the larger high schools in the area," said Joseph.

"I'll call him tomorrow and see what I can find out. Maybe I can go visit one day next week."

"You probably can. Randy said he'd be around all next week and would be glad to meet you."

It wasn't long before Joseph suggested they go get some dinner. "I know you're going to be tired this evening, so you'll want to head over to Rebecca's before it gets too late. Abby has a tennis match this evening, but they'll be back before seven probably," said Joseph.

It was true that Eloise was tired from the trip. She was also looking forward to learning what progress Rebecca had made on wedding preparations. She hadn't realized how many decisions had to be made before a wedding. She was very fortunate to have Rebecca thinking of everything for her.

When they entered the new Outback restaurant where they'd decided to go for dinner, one of the waitresses spoke to Joseph and took them back to a table. As the waitress walked briskly toward the table, a couple at one of the tables stopped Joseph and spoke to him, asking him to introduce "his friend" (meaning Eloise, of course). Eloise learned that the couple go to the same church as Joseph does. They had seen her there a few weeks ago but had not really met her. After a brief conversation, they were seated, and Joseph apologized to the waitress for the delay.

The food was delicious, and it gave Eloise some energy. She enjoyed the meal, and it revived her some, but by the time they got back to Joseph's it was a few minutes after 8:00 p.m., and she was ready to head on over to Rebecca's.

Rebecca and Abby welcomed her as usual. The first thing they wanted to ask about was the possibility of a teaching job that Joseph had told them about. Abby said, "You know I will be going there this fall, don't you?"

"No, I didn't know that. I guess Joseph just left that little bit of information out. But that's great. You can tell me all about the school. You probably know more about it than he does anyway." Abby was smiling.

Rebecca said, "Abby has been so excited since she learned that you might be teaching there. I know you may not actually teach her, but she'll love having you there if you should decide to take the job."

"I'll love having her there too. We can both get integrated into the school together. But you'll probably know a lot of people there, where I'll be totally new," said Eloise.

"Tell us what you're planning to sing at the wedding, Abby," said Rebecca.

"I found this song that I really like," said Abby. "It's called 'At Last,' by Etta James. Are you familiar with it?"

"I've heard the title, but I can't remember the words. Why don't you sing it for me?" said Eloise.

Rebecca moved to the piano and started to play it, while Abby grabbed her sheet music from the top of the piano and began to sing. "*At last my love has come along, my lonely days are over, and my life is like a song....*"

"I love it!" said Eloise.

Wedding plans were going along nicely, but Eloise still wished she had learned what her mother knew about Charles Wright's murder. One morning, she thought about the mention of an older lady who had given them some information. It seemed that Sergeant Jackson had said "most" of her testimony had related to the nurse who'd worked for Charles, but he didn't tell anything else she might have said. Did she know Flo? Was she familiar with Charles' office staff? She decided to call Joseph.

When he answered, she said, "Joseph, do you remember Sergeant Jackson talking about the testimony of an older woman about the Charles Wright case?"

"Yes, I think so," he answered.

"Do you have any idea who that lady was? I was wondering if she knew my mother."

"I don't think he mentioned her name, which makes sense in view of the circumstances," said Joseph. "But she might agree to talk to you."

"Do you think it'd be all right if I called the Sergeant and asked them to see if she'd talk to me?"

"Yes, it's very possible that she could have known your mother. Maybe she could have become acquainted with her when she visited his office. Why don't you call and see. Do you need me to go with you, or call them?"

"Thank you, but I can just call them. If I must talk to her at the station, though, I might want you to go with me."

When Eloise called the station the next morning, Sergeant Jackson said he'd be glad to see if the lady would be willing to talk to her. The sergeant called her back that afternoon, saying that the lady would be glad to talk to her, and that she had suggested they meet at the same little coffee shop Eloise was familiar with. "I didn't ask her if she knew your mother, but I told her who you were and why you were interested in the case," he said and gave her the woman's name and number.

Eloise hoped that this lady might have known her mother, but even if she didn't, it would be good to talk to someone who knew Charles Wright. When she got in touch with the lady—Mrs. Gray was her name—she seemed glad that Eloise had called. "Oh, yes," she said. "I knew your mother well, and I'll be glad to talk to you. You were such a cute little thing, and your mother often brought you to work with her occasionally late in the afternoon. It always fascinated me that you would just play and not bother anyone. Is that little coffee shop okay for us to meet tomorrow?"

"Sure," said Eloise. "What time will you be able to meet me?"

"I often go have some coffee in mid-morning—around 10:00 a.m.— would that be okay?"

"That would be perfect," Eloise said.

When she entered the coffee place, she did not see anyone that she thought would be the lady she was to meet, but it was a little early. She went to the counter and ordered some coffee and a chocolate covered donut to go with it, since she had not eaten breakfast that morning. Then she sat down at the back of the room where she could see the door where customers were coming in. She pulled out her phone and was looking through some emails. Suddenly she heard someone say "Ms. Erickson? Are you Eloise Erickson?" She looked up into the smiling face of an older lady. "Yes, I am. Are you Martha Gray?"

"Yes I am. You have changed a lot," she said, laughing, "but you look so much like your mother that I knew it had to be you." Eloise was not surprised. She thought of the many people who had told her she looked like her mother.

Martha Gray was very friendly, wanting to know where Eloise lived and what she did for a living, and of course, how Flo was. When she learned that Flo had been killed in a car accident, she was shocked. "Oh, I am so sorry. Flo was a wonderful lady, as I'm sure you already know. The first time I met her, we sat and talked for a while, because I had come to see Charles, and it was a while before he returned from lunch. From then on, I felt like she was a friend."

When they began to talk about Charles Wright's death, Eloise said that she knew that Mrs. Gray's testimony had helped them know a little more about what had happened to the nurse, but she hoped that she might know whether Flo knew much about some of the events surrounding both the nurse's death and the murder of Charles Wright.

"Oh, I'm sure she did. She and Charles talked about everything, and the same was true of Charles and the nurse. Now, I don't know exactly what transpired after the nurse's death, but I know that policeman was asking around about what the nurse had talked about with Charles and Flo, because Flo told me he did."

"There is something else I've been curious about that has nothing to do with the murder case," said Eloise. "Initially, I came here to see if I could find out something totally unrelated. As you may already know, I knew nothing about Charles Wright's death. Mother never told me anything about that. The only thing I knew was that my mother's boss while she worked here had paid for my college expenses. I had always thought that he might still be living. I didn't even know about him paying for that until I was in the eleventh grade."

"So, what were you going to do here, honey?"

"Well, at first I came to thank him for doing that, and then of course, I learned that he'd been murdered, but no one had been prosecuted for it, so I got caught up in trying to learn what happened."

Mrs. Gray looked at her. "I am so sorry you never got to meet Charles Wright. Is there anything I can answer for you that has to do with any of it?"

"Probably not. Do you happen to know anything about why he paid for my college, or how that happened?" she asked.

"I don't know exactly why he did it, but I certainly knew he set aside money to pay for it. Your mother was so excited. She said that one day Charles was talking about how smart you were, and then he said that he wanted to be sure you could go to college, so he was putting some money into an account to pay for tuition. She said he figured out how much costs might go up and finally came up with an amount it might cost. I don't have any idea about how much he put into the account of course, but she thought it was a lot of money."

"Oh, you have just answered the question I have pondered over for a long time. I'm sorry I didn't get to thank him, but at least I know he did in fact set aside the money intentionally for my college. I thought it might have just been some money my mother made when she sold her share of the business. I don't know why that was important to me, but it was."

"There's one other thing you should know," said Mrs. Gray. "Your mother left after Charles died because she received a threatening phone call from someone. She said she wasn't going to tell anyone because she didn't trust the police or anyone else after she received the call. That's all I know."

Eloise was relieved because now she felt like she had learned what she needed to know about her mother and about the source of her tuition money. She just wished she'd been able to thank Charles Wright for his help. She couldn't help but feel sad for her mother though, because she realized that her mother must have left Hometown out of fear for her safety. She had never thought much about exactly why her mother had left. Maybe her mother felt much as she had felt when she got that weird call that day.

Mrs. Gray interrupted her thoughts. "I hope I have not upset you by telling you that your mother took you out of this area because of that threatening phone call. I just thought you should know."

"No, I'm glad you told me. You know, I got some threatening phone calls too. I was just thinking what it must have been like for my mother. Fear can make one almost paralyzed. And yet my mother acted quickly to protect me."

"Yes, she did. Your mother was a wonderful person. Don't ever forget that," said Mrs. Gray.

"I won't. I read a book one time by Agatha Christie called *Death Comes as the End*. In it, one of the characters says, 'Fear is incomplete knowledge'. I was just thinking how much of what we've seen in this whole situation demonstrates that. Fear has ruled everything I've tried to do basically ever since my mother died two years ago, and especially since Rebecca and I got those phone calls. And it ruled other people's lives too. Even the policeman who made those calls. He probably would not have called me had he known my mother was dead. You see—incomplete knowledge. And yet, some people are strong enough to go on and live their lives. My mother knew the dangers she faced, and yet she took me away and made a good life for me. It's complicated, but the 'not knowing' seems to be the problem in many situations."

Chapter 17

It was the week before the wedding and most of the work had been done. Eloise was pleased with all the plans that she and Rebecca had made. She was still a little nervous though. She talked to Sophia a few days ago, and although it was obvious that she and Ed were in love with one another, they weren't engaged yet. Eloise knew that Sophia felt that some of his family were prejudiced because she was Mexican.

"I'm still not sure about Ed's family. His cousin made a remark the other day that hurt my feelings. What am I supposed to do about that?"

"Have you talked to Ed about it?" asked Eloise.

"A little. I get the feeling that their family is a little afraid to refute things this cousin says. Maybe his family has a little more wealth or something. I'm not sure what the problem is. It may take a while before I understand exactly what the relationship is between the family members. At this point, I'm just trying to be patient with Ed. I don't think he holds this cousin's views, and I don't think any of his immediate family docs cither. It bothers me a little that they don't speak out, but it seems to be a matter of family dynamics that I don't understand."

"Well, you may want to give him some time to work it out. Often it takes time to understand those family relationships, but you two will probably figure it out."

"I'm not sure. I can't commit to him if he is unwilling to stand up to his cousin, but at the same time, I do love him, and I think he feels the same toward me," said Sophia. "I'm hoping we'll get to talk a little more this weekend. Maybe you and Joseph will inspire him."

"I think you're handling this the right way," said Eloise. "You should not be subjected to his cousin's remarks, but it would help if you understood why Ed's family is so reluctant to confront him. After all, he is not exactly an immediate family member. Maybe Ed will explain it all to you when you have a little more time to talk about it."

The whole thing made Eloise feel sorry for her friend. She was so grateful that Rebecca had accepted her into their family from the beginning. Not only had she welcomed her into the family, but she had been very helpful with the wedding plans. She had arranged for all the reception plans to be carried out by a friend of hers in the church who they could repay after the wedding.

She scheduled her meeting with the principal of the new high school for Wednesday morning at 10:00 a.m. She was both excited and a little fearful. What if they didn't want her after all? What if she didn't want to take the job if they offered it to her? "Calm down," she told herself. "It's probably going to be fine, and if it isn't, you'll be able to deal with it."

By the time she turned into the school parking lot, she had pulled herself together, and decided that one way or another, she would make a decision. If the decision turned out to be the wrong one, she could decide to do something else.

The receptionist smiled when Eloise entered the office. "You must be Ms. Erickson, the soon-to-be bride of Joseph Wright," she said. "Randy will be with you in a moment. Just have a seat."

About five minutes later, the principal walked out of his office. Randy Manis was an average-sized man with a big smile and a confident expression. "Ms. Erickson, I am so glad to meet you. I know you're a nice person, because you plan to marry one of my best friends. Come on into my office."

After he told her a little about the school and answered some of her questions, he began to tell her about the job opening he was hoping she might be able to fill. "I know that you have been teaching English III, so you should be comfortable with that. The position includes three sections of English III, but I also need someone to teach two sections of journalism. English III will be similar to the one you've taught before—it is Honors English. It is only slightly different from the IB curriculum with which you are familiar. In the two journalism classes, you'll have a little more freedom to be innovative."

"I have not had experience teaching journalism, but I did take several courses in the field in college. Tell me a little about what is expected in those classes."

"The only thing that might be a little different is that these classes also produce our school newspaper. Different newspaper advisors have handled it in different ways," said Randy. "One teacher set it up so that one section worked on the newspaper and the other just studied how to write news stories, editorials, and so on. Another teacher actually had both sections produce part of the paper. I think one did only news articles and the other did editorials, and she chose the best ones to put in the paper. We can talk about how these different approaches worked for them if you decide you are willing to teach those classes."

"Are you saying that if I teach here, I'd choose one of those approaches?"

"Not necessarily. I also thought about having Journalism I and II, and letting the Journalism II class be for those that had already had the course and having them run the newspaper. For those who haven't had Journalism I, they would begin there and would not be responsible for the paper. I'm sorry, I realize I'm rambling. What do you think? Or do you even want to do this?"

"This sounds like my ideal job! Of course, I would need some help in understanding what has been done before, and not doing anything rash, but I have loved teaching English III in an Honors program, and I like journalism. I was advising the yearbook staff at the school in Nashville, but I'd only done it one year."

After the discussion, Randy asked Eloise if she'd like a short tour of the facility, just to get an idea of what it was like, and she said she would love to have a tour. Eloise was pleased to see that the building was clean and looked well-kept. The classrooms looked inviting, and she liked where the English wing was located.

When she was ready to leave, Randy gave her copies of the textbooks she'd be using that fall. "Well, I guess I'll see you Saturday then," he said.

"Of course," she said. "I hope I haven't seemed too scattered today, but I've had so many decisions to make these last few weeks that I'm almost crazy."

"No, you're doing fine," he said. "I look forward to working with you."

When she called Joseph later that day, they were both happy with her decision.

One thing that neither Rebecca nor Eloise had thought about was that there would be no one to walk down the aisle with her at the wedding. The only person she thought about was a person who had been dead for years. Under different circumstances, Charles Wright would have been the perfect person to walk her down the aisle. At first, Eloise panicked at the thought that there was no one, but later she realized that many young women have been in that position. Walking down the aisle alone was not really a problem. She'd just do it! It was true that she'd lost a lot of people who were family, but now she was becoming family to some wonderful people—Joseph, Rebecca, and Abby. Also, she would develop wonderful relationships with Jane and her husband, and those two adorable little boys. Family comes in all kinds of ways.

That night after Joseph left, Rebecca looked at Eloise. "You'll never know how important you've become to me over the last few months. You know, after my divorce, I was so lonely, and then after Abby began to grow up a little, that helped some, but I felt like I was still somewhat of a burden on Joseph. In fact, I felt that maybe I was in some way responsible for his break-up with that girl he was dating, although he always insisted that I wasn't. Then when you and I met at the little coffee shop that day, I really felt a connection with you. I hate to tell you this, but part of me didn't want to share you with Joseph, because I was afraid he'd take you away. In a way, I guess he did, but after the two of you met, I could tell there was something good between you, and I wanted him to have that. I felt like we both had suffered from the same thing—loneliness. The thing is though, that even though you two are getting married, I feel as though I'm gaining a family member, so I'm happy for both of you."

"We are both gaining a family member, Rebecca," said Eloise. "I felt it the first time I met you, especially after I came here and met Abby. I think we're going to be family, the kind that loves and supports one another."

"Maybe I shouldn't tell you this—I haven't even told Joseph. But recently I've met a special person that just might be the right one for me. Like you, it's been a while, so I'm rather skeptical. You know I work most weekends at the hospital." Eloise nodded. "Well about two months ago, we got a new doctor there. For some reason he seemed to notice me, and single me out to ask me about certain procedures or patients. Two weeks ago, as I was leaving the hospital one Sunday morning, he was also leaving, and he asked me if I'd like to get a cup of coffee before going home. I learned that he was divorced with a daughter close to Abby's age. We talked for a long time, and it was the weirdest thing. I felt more comfortable with him than I'd felt with anyone since my divorce. I left the coffee shop feeling like there might be hope. The other thing is that Abby knows his daughter. Now I've not said anything to her about the doctor, but Abby has made some positive comments about the girl, so again, it gives me hope."

"I think I know how you feel. That's the way I felt when I met Joseph. You hope, but then you're afraid to hope," said Eloise.

"He actually called me last weekend because I wasn't working, and of course I'm not working this weekend either. But he asked me to go to dinner next Thursday. I said yes," she said, with a sly smile.

"They say that good things come to those who are willing to wait," said Eloise. "Maybe that's what we're both learning this year."

"Even if this thing with the doctor doesn't work out, I believe the fact that you and Joseph have gotten together has given me an additional family member. It gives me great joy to see him happier than he's been in years."

"I hope it works out for you, and for him of course," said Eloise. "It sounds like you have a lot in common—with the girls and with your careers both being in medicine," said Eloise. "May I tell Joseph about this?"

"I guess so," said Rebecca. "It's possible that someone else will see us at the restaurant and tell him. If you tell him, then he won't be surprised if that should happen."

Chapter 18

When Eloise awoke on Saturday morning, the first thing she saw was her wedding dress hanging on the back of the door across the room. When she finally realized it was her wedding day, she sat up in bed. Her heart was beating way too fast. It really is today, she thought. All the talking about it and planning for it had been done, and the day had come. By tonight, she'd be Mrs. Joseph Wright. She'd be a member of the Wright family. As she contemplated that, she was grateful that she'd helped learn what had happened to Charles Wright. Maybe she hadn't done much, but still in some small way she'd helped. It might never have happened if she had not decided to come here and tried to look into her past a bit. She thought that her mother might be proud of her for doing that.

She put on her bath robe and walked down the stairs and into the kitchen, where she found Rebecca and Abby having breakfast.

"Oh, there's the bride!" said Abby. "How're you feeling? No panic or regret, I hope."

"Nope. You're not getting rid of me that easy, girlie," said Eloise.

"I don't think either of us want to get rid of you. We're just hoping you won't dump us! I need a sister, and Abby needs an auntie," said Rebecca.

"Well, it won't be long then," said Eloise.

"What time do we have to be at the church?" asked Abby.

"I think we're meeting at 1:00 p.m. for everyone to get dressed and take pictures of the bride and Maid of Honor," said Rebecca.

Abby said, "Okay, and I'm going to work with the ministers and musicians to get the ceremony stuff all worked out at 1:00 p.m., and then you and I will come back home to change just before the wedding. Is that right?"

"That's right," said Rebecca. "I'll be at the church while the bride and Maid of Honor are getting dressed, and then when the photographers come to take pictures, we'll come back and get dressed here."

They all ate a hearty breakfast, and Rebecca spent most of the rest of the morning making phone calls, answering calls, and helping Eloise get everything together that she needed to take to the church. The beautician came at 9:00 a.m. to fix Eloise's, Sophia's, and Abby's hair, so there was not time for a proper lunch. They had to eat as they could find time. Rebecca had prepared some easy-to-manage sandwiches and put them on the table in the kitchen, where there were drinks and some chips. It was chaotic, but it worked well. By 12:30 p.m., Eloise and Sophia were on their way to the church, followed by Rebecca and Abby.

About an hour and a half before the wedding, Rebecca gave some instructions to the photographers and other helpers before she and Abby left the church and headed home to get dressed for the wedding.

As the pre-service music played, Eloise's nerves were on high alert, and she began to think about having to walk down the aisle—alone. Sophia looked beautiful as she walked down the aisle, escorted by Joseph's Best Man. Apparently, she had met him in the foyer and they seemed to have an understanding about what they were to do.

When they got almost down to the alter, Eloise felt like she might faint. Then she thought of her mother, who always said, "Everything's going to be all right." Then she felt the presence of both her mother and of Charles Wright, who had wanted her to be able to go to college. She thought of Joseph, the love of her life. Suddenly, she felt calm and well-loved. When it was her turn to walk down the aisle, she did so without hesitation. She was ready to become Mrs. Joseph Wright.

Once she joined the others at the front of the sanctuary, she knew she'd be all right. As Abby stood and sang and the ceremony progressed, she felt extremely grateful for her life. The ceremony was beautiful, and the small crowd seemed to enfold her in a strong embrace. She and Joseph exchanged their vows and a short time later they were pronounced husband and wife. As they exited the sanctuary, and the audience members were invited next door for the reception, it seemed like she had taken on a new life—and she had. The photographers needed a few more pictures, posed at the altar, of the couple with the minister, etc. Soon, they entered the reception to loud applause and spent some time visiting with friends and accepting congratulations from the crowd.

Their plan was to spend the night at Joseph's house and then leave Sunday morning for a short trip to Hawaii. Their flight was for 12:00 p.m. on Sunday, so they were not pressed for time. The trip was designed to be relaxing and enjoyable. Although they had not planned a long trip, it was adequate and just what they both needed. Rebecca and Abby came to see them off the next morning, bringing some crackers and chips for snacks on the plane. "We knew they wouldn't allow drinks or any kind of fruit, so this was all we could think of that would be allowed," said Abby.

The trip was fun, and when they returned they were rested and ready to settle into a new routine.

Chapter 19

Sophia and Ed had seemed to be happy at the wedding, but Eloise kept thinking about the tension regarding his cousin's attitude toward Mexicans. She did not have time to discuss anything with Sophia when she came to the wedding, so she had no idea how things were going between them. She'd hoped that the wedding would make a positive impact on both of them, but she knew that it was unlikely to change things. She knew that Sophia had planned to talk to him about it when they made the trip over to her wedding, but she had no way of knowing if they even talked about it. Even if they talked about it, things might not have improved. About three weeks after the wedding, Sophia called Eloise.

"I'm so glad you called," Eloise told her. "I've thought about you a lot since the wedding. How are things going?"

"Oh, I just had to let you know that Ed and I had a long talk on our way home after your wedding. He was so impressed with the wedding. When we started back, he asked me to marry him. I told him that I could not commit to marry him with his cousin continuing to make snide remarks about my people and getting no push-back from him or anyone in his immediate family. He seemed surprised at first, and I learned that his cousin's side of the family had always had a little more money and had been a little more educated. Because of that, Ed's family had always hesitated to confront them about anything. I told him that was his family's choice, but I didn't want to put up with it, so I wasn't going to marry into a family where I was treated that way and everyone just accepted it."

"So, did you all break up then?" asked Eloise.

"Well, he said he was sorry I felt that way, but he didn't think there was anything he could do about it. Of course, I knew he could speak up if he wanted to, so I just said 'okay'. I thought that's the last I'd see of him."

"Well, was it?"

"No," said Sophia. "The next day, he called me. He said he'd talked to his family and told them that he wanted to marry me, and that if they would not confront his cousin, and did not want him to, that he and I would not be visiting them and would not invite them to our wedding if we had one."

"Wow! That's a pretty strong man right there!" said Eloise.

"Yes. And the other thing I wanted to tell you is—we're engaged!"

"Congratulations! Have you set the date yet?"

"No, but it's probably going to be next spring. We went over to his house last week, and his parents both apologized to me and told me that they hadn't realized how much it hurt me for the guy to say those things, and they didn't even realize that he'd said some of the things he had said. They had actually told him a few days before that they did not agree with the way he'd spoken to me, and that he wouldn't be welcome there if he continued to talk that way."

When she ended the call with Sophia, Eloise was so happy for her. She was also glad that Sophia was strong enough to stand her ground and tell Ed that she would not marry him if he could not stand up to his cousin. That was important for her to do. She was excited for Sophia.

She had not seen Rebecca much after she and Joseph had come back from Hawaii. She knew that Rebecca had been seeing the doctor she'd mentioned earlier, but Eloise had been so busy getting settled into her own new life with Joseph that she had little time for anything else.

She knew that once school started, she wouldn't have time to do all those little things she needed to do in the kitchen and bedroom. She and Joseph had decided to get new bedding and window coverings for the bedroom. She also wanted to put new shelf liners in the kitchen, and she wanted to replace a few of the everyday dishes that were missing. Joseph had said that if she couldn't get them replaced, she could just replace all of them, but she was hoping to find some just like the ones they had.

One day, amidst all the little errands Eloise had to run, she decided to go by Rebecca's and see how she and Abby were doing. It was about 11:00 a.m. and she thought they might both be home. Rebecca came to the door. "Oh, look who's here, Abby!" she said, loud enough so Abby could hear her.

"I just had to see how you were doing. I haven't had much time to keep up. I've been doing a lot of little things around the house. Joseph helps in the evenings, but I do all the errands during the daytime."

"Come on in," said Rebecca. "I've been wanting to talk to you."

Abby came bounding down the stairs. "Oh, it's Auntie!"

"I've missed both of you. It's good to see you. I've barely seen you since the wedding," said Eloise. "But I've thought about what a good job you did. Rebecca, you did a lot of work planning the whole thing, and Abby, everyone seemed enthralled with your beautiful singing."

"We got your sweet note," said Rebecca. "And we really appreciate it. It all went well, didn't it?"

"Joseph and I thought it was perfect," said Eloise. "By the way, are you still seeing the doctor that you told me about?"

"Well, yes we've gone out several times," said Rebecca,

"Can I tell her about tonight, Mama?" Interrupted Abby.

"I guess so," said Rebecca, "especially since you've already got her interested."

"The doctor and his daughter, who is almost my age, are coming over to have dinner with us tonight. Mama and I are cooking for them."

"Oh, that's great. What are you fixing for dinner?"

"Pork loin, potatoes, green beans . . ." Abby went on to describe all the dishes they were serving.

"That all sounds good," said Eloise.

"Mama's all nervous because it's his first time coming to eat with us, but I'm excited because my friend's coming."

"What's her name?" asked Eloise.

"Oh, I'm sorry. Her name is Valerie," said Abby.

"She's seems really sweet," said Rebecca. "Her mother and dad have been divorced since she was in preschool, I think, but she's always lived with her dad."

"She told me she doesn't remember much about her mother," said Abby.

Later, Rebecca told Eloise that Valerie's mother had just left them when Valerie was five, and he didn't even hear from her for about six months. He went ahead and got custody after six months. After that he did hear from her a couple of times, but she never tried to share custody or anything like that. He told Rebecca that she never even asked about Valerie.

Eloise learned that although Valerie had never had problems at home or school that her dad said he felt that her mother leaving had left her scarred in many ways. Rebecca seemed anxious to get to know her and try to repair some of the damage that had been done.

In the subsequent weeks, Rebecca and Eloise talked often, and it was apparent that Rebecca was getting attached to the young girl. Abby was too. It was not uncommon for Valerie to come home with Abby for all three of them to meet her dad for dinner when he finished work, or for her dad to come to Rebecca's for dinner. Eloise was somewhat concerned that Valerie would become too attached to Rebecca and Abby and then the doctor would break up with Rebecca. She was afraid that it would be damaging to Valerie. She'd asked Rebecca about it once, but she didn't seem to be worried about it, Eloise ended up feeling like she was meddling in their business, so she said no more.

It was just a week before school started. Eloise had met some of the teachers she would be working with and she and one of them had to go by the superintendent's office to pick up some supplies they'd need. While they were there, of course she went in to see Joseph. They talked a few minutes and then he said, "Rebecca said she was going to call you tonight."

"All right. I haven't talked to her for a few weeks. Is she okay?"

"I think so. She didn't exactly say why she was calling you, but I'm pretty sure she's fine."

"Great. I'll look forward to talking to her," said Eloise.

It was about 7:00 p.m. when she got the call from Rebecca. After they chatted a bit, Rebecca said, "I called because I've got some exciting news. Scott and I are engaged. We're getting married this fall sometime. We haven't set a date yet."

"Oh, I'm so happy for you. Congratulations! What does Valerie say about that?"

"She's thrilled. Do you know what she said to her dad? She said, 'Dad, what took you so long? Abby and I have been ready for months!' I just love her, and I want to be a mom whom she can count on to always be there," said Rebecca.

"That's wonderful. I hope I can be of help to you during this time. Just let me know if there is anything I can do to help," said Eloise.

The following weekend, Eloise and Joseph drove over to Nashville to pick up the few things she'd left in her old apartment. While there, they spent some time with Sophia and her fiancé Ed. It seemed as if they'd worked out all their problems and were happily planning their wedding. Of course, she had already asked Eloise to be her Maid of Honor, but her two sisters were going to be bridesmaids, and Ed's brother would be his Best Man. Some of his friends at work would be in the wedding and would escort her sisters down the aisle. The wedding was scheduled for close to Christmas.

Most of the weekend, Sophia and Eloise were not alone, but on Saturday afternoon they stayed at Sophia's apartment while the guys ran some errands. Eloise asked Sophia how her mother and sisters' were doing.

"Maria and Ana are fine, but Mama has been having some problems. She's supposed to go to the doctor Monday. I'm not sure what they'll find," said Sophia. Eloise saw that her eyes were a little teary.

"Oh, I hope it isn't serious."

"I'm going with her to the doctor Monday. She thinks it's nothing, but I don't know."

"Please call me when you learn anything. I love your mother," Eloise told her.

She was glad that she and Joseph had decided to stay in the hotel, since Sophia's mother wasn't feeling well. Initially, Gabriela had invited them to stay with her, but they declined, mainly because they weren't sure when they would arrive. Also, Gabriela lived a good way out from the area where Eloise had lived and she thought the hotel would be easier to get to where she needed to go. She loved Sophia's mother, though, and wished she could have seen her.

When they returned home that weekend, Eloise and Joseph were both glad to be back. "I'm so glad I chose to live here instead of Nashville," she said. "This just feels like home to me."

"Me, too," said Joseph, laughing. "Now that Rebecca has found someone, I feel like we are all home."

"Yes," said Eloise. "For so long, I felt like I had no home. Even though Mother and I lived in Nashville for most of my life, I must have sensed her uncertainty or something. All that time I guess she felt as if something might happen, and those people would find her. I don't know. She always seemed a little uneasy in some ways."

"I forgot to ask you about meeting with that Mrs. Gray that had provided some information to the police about the nurse who worked for Charles Wright. Did you learn anything new?"

"As a matter of fact, I did. She verified the fact that Mr. Wright had wanted to provide for my college education and that he'd set up an account to do that. "Apparently from what she told me, Martha Gray actually knew my mother quite well," said Eloise. "I'd forgotten that you did not know what she said. As soon as she saw me, she said I looked a lot like my mom, and she would have known me because of that."

"Well, things seem to be coming together for both you and Rebecca," said Joseph. "It makes me so happy that Rebecca and that doctor got together. They have a lot in common, don't they?"

"Yes. And both their daughters seem to be happy about it too," said Eloise. "I believe that's a winning romance."

Eloise spent the last few days of summer finishing up a few changes she'd wanted to make in her new home. She loved the extra space in her kitchen. It made her want to spend more time there. The changes were mainly rearranging things in the cabinets and pantry, not redesigning anything. She liked the soft green and grey colors of the cabinets and the walls, and she loved the appliances, which were all stainless steel. Joseph said he had asked an interior designer to come in and make suggestions when he bought the house, which needed updating. "I knew nothing about what needed to be done, but it was pretty obvious something was needed. I knew that an interior designer would give me a few good options," he said.

"I knew you were a smart man," said Eloise.

Joseph encouraged her to make any changes she felt were needed to improve things, especially in the kitchen. "You know I don't spend a lot of time cooking, so I may have overlooked some major flaws," he had said, laughing.

It didn't take her long to feel right at home in that kitchen. Before the summer was over, she was spending much of her day experimenting with different recipes and enjoying cooking more than ever before.

The night before the first day of school that fall, Eloise called Rebecca. "Do you want me to pick up Abby in the morning so you won't have to get out as early?"

"As far as I know, she was expecting me to take her, but if you'd be willing to do that, it'd be okay with me," said Rebecca. "Let me see what she says."

A few minutes later, Rebecca came back on the phone, saying, "Well, of course, she'd rather ride with her *auntie* than with me!"

That became a regular morning routine, Eloise pulling up in the driveway and Abby running out the door to greet her. It was a little earlier than Rebecca had always taken her to school, but she seemed to love spending time with Eloise, and of course, Eloise loved spending time with her favorite ninth grade student. Most of the time they rode home together. If one of them had to stay at school late, Rebecca would occasionally pick Abby up, but most of the time it worked out fine.

Finally, thought Eloise, she really had a family, like many of her friends and co-workers over the years had, and she felt right at home in Hometown, with no fear of the unknown.

Thinking back over the last few years, Eloise realized that fear had ruled her life in many ways, and she thought about that story she had read a few years ago by Agatha Christie called *Death Comes as the End*. She didn't remember much about the book, but she remembered again that statement one of the characters had made: "Fear is incomplete knowledge." As she thought about the quote, she knew that she had feared so many things, especially since her mother had died, and it seemed that fear was a factor in many people's lives. She realized that having family and community support is the key to living a happy life.

Acknowledgements

I want to begin by thanking Martha Heneisen for her encouragement in writing, as well as her willingness to read and give feedback on all my novels. I also want to thank Sharon McBrayer for reading and providing feedback for several of my novels, including this one. Thank you to Deborah Malone, a fellow writer who has had much experience in writing mysteries, for giving me feedback on this novel. Thanks also to my husband Bill, who has been the first reader for every novel I've written, and always provided good feedback. I also want to thank Irene Bennett for reading the novel and writing a blurb, as well as giving some helpful suggestions for improvement. Last, but not least, I want to thank Linda Davies, my sister-in-law, for encouraging me to write the story.

www.ingramcontent.com/pod-product-compliance
Lightning Source LLC
Chambersburg PA
CBHW061523050726
47503CB00015B/2690